The Tale of Sir Gawain

The Tale of Sir Gawain

Neil Philip

Illustrated by
Charles Keeping

Philomel Books
NEW YORK

Library of Congress Cataloging-in-Publication Data
Philip, Neil.   The tale of Sir Gawain.
   Summary: The knight Gawain recounts the adventures of
King Arthur and his fellow members of the Round Table, his
own battle with the Green Knight, his marriage, and the final
days before the fall of Camelot.
   1. Gawain (Legendary character)—Romances.   2. Arthu-
rian romances.   [1. Gawain (Legendary character) 2. Arthur,
King.   3. Folklore—England.   4. Knights and knight-
hood—Folklore]   I. Keeping, Charles, ill.   II. Title.
PZ8.1.P55Tal   1987   398.2'2'0942   87-6997
ISBN 0-399-21488-7

CONTENTS

Genealogical Table

I
· The Knights of the Round Table · 1

II
· The Sword in the Stone · 6

III
· Sir Owain and the Lady of the Fountain · 15

IV
· Sir Gawain and the Green Knight · 28

V
· The Marriage of Sir Gawain · 39

VI
· The Fair Unknown · 47

VII
· Sir Perceval · 55

VIII
· The Quest for the Holy Grail · 65

IX
· The Holy Grail · 72

X
· Lancelot and Guinevere · 78

XI
· The Banishment of Lancelot ·   89

XII
· Return to England ·   94

XIII
· The Death of Gawain ·   96

· Postscript ·   100

· Author's Note on Sources ·   102

GENEALOGICAL TABLE

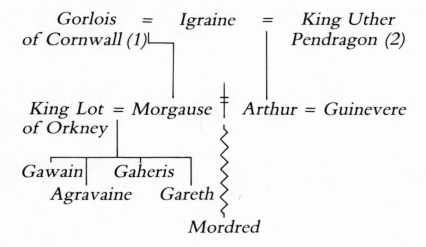

1

The Knights of the Round Table

Think. Think. I can't think. The brain is bathed in blood. In blood. I try to think, but all my memories are broken.

Boy, boy, don't go away. Let me speak. It helps me if I speak. If only I could get it all clear.

I'm going to tell it all to you. Perhaps it will make a pattern. Write it down. I like to see you write. I was never much of a fist at that. You write it down. It must make sense. It must.

My head works so.

Lancelot was my best friend. Before all this. Perhaps he was the only one who didn't need anything from me. The others kept their distance. I was cross-grained, and I sat too close to the king. Too close. The king's my uncle, you know that, boy? But of course you do. Of course.

It's cold in this tent. Build up the fire.

I swear my wits have spilled from my skull where Lancelot split it open. My thoughts go round in circles,

1

circles, like the snake on Guinevere's ring that's biting its own tail.

Why does Lancelot play with me? He may think it generous to spare my life. I spit on his generosity. He wasn't so nice with my brothers Gareth and Gaheris. He made that yard a shambles when he rescued the queen. He cut my brothers to pieces. They had no weapons. They loved that man. And now he says he didn't see them. Well, he sees me. He's only to look over his castle wall to see me. And I'll stay here till one of us is dead.

Oh Lancelot, Lancelot.

He was the pride of us all. You should have seen him as a young man. He was so strong, and so gentle in his strength. He was kind to my little brother Gareth when Gareth was just a kitchen boy, and the others sneered and called Gareth "Pretty Hands".

Ay, but he knew no kindness when he rescued Guinevere from the king's justice. He was among the king's men like a wolf among sheep, or a hawk among sparrows. And he slew my brothers who loved him and would not bear arms against him, not even for the king.

I was watching, boy. I was watching from the window, at the king my uncle's side. I watched them bring the queen out in her shift to be burnt. I watched them tie her to the stake. The king was looking, but he didn't see. His eyes were thick with tears. He's always loved her, that poor foolish woman. Her and Lancelot both. They meant more to him, I think, than his kingdom or his crown. Certainly more than his pride. But he is king. When my brother Agravaine - the Devil skewer him - forced the secret of their guilty love on him, he had to act. Long years he held his peace, but in the end, he had to act. And don't think him cruel, to try to burn his dear. There were those who wanted her tied between four horses and torn apart: that was the old way. Ay, that was the old way.

And when Lancelot rode in, my heart leapt with joy within me. With joy. I knew he'd not let her burn, while the breath of life was in him. But to lay about him as he did! He must have been mad. Perhaps he is mad. Perhaps we are all mad. Our brains are all turned the wrong way.

I went into the yard. My brothers were lying at the foot of the fire that had been built. They looked... they looked almost peaceful, asleep. But there was something broken about their mouths. I called them. "Gareth! Gaheris!" I called them. But they were the length of my shout from me.

And I swore, I swore by the sun, the moon and the stars, by the earth below me, the sky above me and the sea around me, not to rest till Lancelot was dead. I cursed his hand that struck my brothers down. I curse it now. For the death of Sir Gareth, for the death of Sir Gaheris, I would hunt Sir Lancelot through the kingdoms of seven kings. I will kill him if I can. May my heart be cut from my body before I forgive him.

So here we are, boy, camped outside his wall, and Arthur's army all around us. Listen! You can hear the horses snorting and stamping, the soldiers dicing and shouting, someone singing. But I, boy, I can hear Lancelot breathing. In, out, in, out, like the beat of my own heart, like the crash and suck of the waves on the shore. And every breath is one breath nearer his doom. One breath nearer his doom.

I've no quarrel with the queen. There's too little fondness in the world to hate because other people love. I stood by when the king took her back, and let Lancelot scuttle free to this castle in France. Let the king and the queen, and Lancelot, and the Pope and all the bishops in Christendom swear blind that black is white; I'll not gainsay them.

The queen was never beautiful, you know. Not the beauty that sets young lads mooning. But she was always so alive. She moved slowly, lazily almost, but there was something, a tension in her, like a filly about to bolt, that was the opposite of lazy. There was something wild in her she was holding fast. And when Lancelot was by, she tightened her grip. You could see it in her face when he was near. Her bones would push up from her cheeks and her nostrils would flare. Sometimes, her eyes seemed to be spilling light; and sometimes they were so black it was as if there was nothing behind them. Yet with the king, they stayed an even grey.

. And then she let go of whatever it was she was holding inside her, and Sir Lancelot let go, and through their love the noble fellowship of the Round Table was broken for ever.

Well, it's all history now. I'll tell you another day.

She must be lonely tonight, the queen, in England. Everything she loves is here. Lancelot. Arthur. Me too, boy, me too. She always had a merry word for me. And now we're all at each other's throats. She knows it's her doing. That's cold comfort on a night as bitter as this.

I worry about her. I worry about England, in Mordred's keeping. Ay: Mordred is Regent. Did you not know? The king's bastard by his own half-sister, my mother. Mordred the viper.

If I had the energy, I could hate Mordred. But there's no room in me for anything but this anger, that burns in me, burns me like a fever. There's nothing but the fire, and the taste of ashes, ashes on my tongue. Why should that be?

Leave me now. Go, go! I need to sleep. But I can't sleep. Lancelot breathes so loud, so loud. But go.

11

The Sword in the Stone

Who's there?

Oh, it's you, boy. Come and sit by me. I want to tell you about the start of all this.

When Uther Pendragon was king of England, he had an adviser called Merlin, an enchanter, a dream reader. And Merlin helped Uther commit a great crime, a crime against my family. For Uther fell in love with my mother's mother, Igraine, though Igraine was married to my grandfather, Gorlois Duke of Cornwall. Uther fell in love, and Merlin by his black and secret arts helped him kill Gorlois and seduce Igraine. Merlin put a spell on Uther's appearance, and Igraine thought she was in bed with her husband, while Gorlois lay cold on the battlefield. And when she knew she was going to have a baby, Igraine could do nothing but marry Uther, and be his queen.

Merlin... No man ever really knew who Merlin was, or what he wanted. Some say he was the devil's son.

Certainly that trick on Igraine was the devil's work, and Merlin made a devil's bargain for it. For the price he asked for his spell was nothing less than the child, when it was born. He took the squalling bundle when it was but a few hours old. Uther threatened and Igraine pleaded, but there was nothing they could do. They had to watch their baby disappear into the pelting rain, no one knew where. The wind howled round Uther's castle that night. It howled.

Men cursed Merlin when Uther died, for Igraine had had no more sons. For ten lean years, England had no king. Throughout my childhood, men like my father, King Lot, were gnawing at the borders of Uther's kingdom, stealing a patch of land here, a whole county there. My father in particular felt he had the right, for he had married one of Gorlois and Igraine's dark and subtle daughters, Morgause, and had by her four sons: myself, Agravaine, Gaheris and Gareth. For my mother and her sister Morgan, it was a sweet delight to see Uther's land despoiled.

It seemed that the whole of England would collapse into a group of squabbling little kingdoms. Outlaws and evil men of all kinds flourished. No one was safe. And even those who had heard of Uther and Igraine's child dismissed it as a story.

Then, one Christmas Day, Merlin reappeared, and caused a great stone to appear in a London churchyard. Set in the stone was an anvil, and sticking out of the top of the anvil was a sword. There were letters inscribed in gold upon its hilt, and they read, "Whoso pulleth out this sword from this stone and anvil is rightwise king born of all England".

Tongues began to wag at that. But once all the jokers had tried and failed to remove the sword, it was decided to call a tournament for New Year's Day. Every knight in the kingdom would come; surely one of them would prove to be the king. But when the day came, not one of the knights could budge the sword an inch.

When all had tried and failed to pull the sword from the stone, the knights moved on to challenge each other on the tournament field. One of these knights was a young man from the north of England, Sir Kay. Now Sir Kay was a hasty and ill-tempered youth, and when he reached the tournament field and realised he'd forgotten his sword, his young squire, a lad about your age – what, thirteen or fourteen? – got the blame. Kay cuffed him, and shouted at him, and sent him running to fetch it.

But when the lad arrived at the house where they were lodging, he found everything locked and barred. Everyone was at the jousting. So he had no choice but to make his way back to Sir Kay, empty-handed. On the way back, though, he passed a churchyard, and in that churchyard he saw the very thing he wanted sticking right through the anvil into a stone: a sword. He didn't pause or think, but just took the sword and carried it to Sir Kay.

Now Sir Kay was no fool – he was never that – and he knew at once by the writing on the hilt what it was the squire had brought him. He called his father Sir Ector to his side, and said, "Here is the sword from the stone. I am the rightful king of England."

Sir Ector just looked at Kay. And then he led his son back to the churchyard, and into the church. Then he took a bible and gave it to Kay, saying, "Son, swear to me on this holy book that you yourself removed the sword."

"My squire Arthur brought it to me," said Sir Kay.

So Sir Ector called the lad Arthur into the church, and asked him how he came by the sword. Arthur thought he was to be scolded, and seizing the weapon he ran to slide it back through the anvil into the stone. He said he hadn't meant to do wrong.

Sir Ector and Sir Kay followed Arthur back into the churchyard, and they both tugged at the sword, but it would not move. "Arthur," said Sir Ector, "remove the sword again," and Arthur withdrew it as easily as from a scabbard. Then Sir Ector and Sir Kay knelt down before him, and kissed his hand. And Arthur, who had been raised as a foster brother to Sir Kay, said, "Father, brother, why do you kneel to me?"

Sir Ector told him, 'I am not your father, Arthur, nor is Sir Kay your brother. You are a foundling child, brought to me as a baby by the enchanter Merlin. Since then, I have raised you as my own. I never dreamed you were King Uther's son."

Then, boy, the lad Arthur wept, because Sir Ector was not his father, and Sir Kay was not his brother, and he was king of all England.

You can imagine the nobles and the knights were not well pleased. But not one of them could move the sword, and Arthur could do so whenever he pleased. It was the common folk - the ones who suffered most from the lawlessness of the times and the caprice of the nobles who thought everything they did was right because they did it - it was the common folk who made Arthur king.

And when he was king, it was the common folk Arthur helped most. With Kay as his steward, and Merlin as his guide, he set about restoring law and justice to the land. And to help him do so, he created the fellowship of the Knights of the Round Table, for those knights who wanted to fight wrong, and help him rule justly and wisely.

There were a hundred and fifty seats at that table, but not a hundred and fifty knights to sit at it. Arthur had barely a handful he could really trust. But Merlin foresaw it all. As each man took his seat, his name would appear on his chair in letters of gold - set there, maybe, before he was even born.

9

But before those seats could be filled, Arthur had to fight the kings, such as my father, who had grown fat on the pickings of his kingdom when it had no king. Eleven kings banded against him, thinking him an upstart, the puppet of that devil's spawn Merlin. There was King Lot, my father. There was old King Clarivans of Northumberland; Idris of Cornwall; Ryens of North Wales; Carados; and half a dozen more whose names I've forgotten, though I can see their faces still. Brutal faces, for the most part.

"King" is just a name some folk give the man with the strongest fist and the loudest voice. Arthur is different. My father, too. He had his code. But some of them! There was one, a king without a kingdom, a robber and scavenger who just called himself The King with a Hundred Knights. He'd have cut my father's throat without a qualm if it suited his purpose. But my father had to take what allies he could get. They fell on England like a pack of slavering dogs on a bone. And just like dogs, if one had seized the bone the others would have fought him for it.

I was there at the great battle of Bedgrayne, where Arthur crushed those kings like so many lice beneath his jacket. It was Merlin's art that did it, for Merlin brought King Ban and King Bors secretly from France, and they pounced on my father's troops from behind like cats on a mouse.

That was a terrible slaughter, that day at Bedgrayne. They say Merlin watched it all from his great black horse, all the killing that stemmed from the day he gave Uther Pendragon the face and figure of Gorlois of Cornwall to satisfy his lust. And Merlin muttered, "It is never done. Is this not enough? Of sixty thousand men this day, not fifteen thousand are left alive." Then he shouted, and every man on that battlefield heard him: "Hold your swords, for the love of God!"

Merlin's eyes filled with darkness. He seemed giddy, restless, frenzied, unsteady. He leapt from his horse, and shouted "Merlin is a bird! Merlin is a bird!", and ran off into the woods, flapping his arms for all the world as if he thought he was flying.

There was no more killing that day.

After that, Merlin was lost to Arthur's court. Every now and then someone would catch a glimpse of him, high in the branches of a tree, prophesying and ranting. In all England there was no plain, field or bare mountain, no bog or thicket or marsh, not a hill nor hollow nor dense-sheltering wood he did not travel, living alone, feasting on apples, with only a pig for company. He seemed to those who saw him an uncouth, famished madman: horrible, fearful, stark naked.

"Listen, little pig," he would say. "Last night I never slept. The snow crept up to my knees, icicles formed in my beard, and all night I watched the moon, and saw the stars dance patterns in the sky. Today I will tell you what the stars told me." And then he would prophesy, telling all that was to happen to Arthur and to England, in the years to come.

They tell me he foretold all this, that we are living through. I paid no attention at the time. I never wanted to know the hour of my death before it came upon me.

It's said some men once tried to prove that Merlin's prophecies were simply the lies of a mad fool, so they brought a boy to him and asked, "Merlin, how will this boy die?" And Merlin replied, "Falling from a high rock." Then the men took the boy away, cut off his hair and brought him back, asking, "Merlin, how will *this* boy die?" And Merlin answered, "Hanging in a tree." Then they took the boy away again and dressed him in a girl's clothes, and brought him back, asking, "Merlin, how will this girl die?" And Merlin said, "Girl or no, drowning in the river." The men laughed, and pelted Merlin with stones, and called him names. That very week, the boy stumbled when out hunting. He fell from a high rock, his feet caught in the branches of a riverside tree and he hung with his head beneath the water until he drowned. So he suffered all three deaths.

Merlin recovered his wits at last, by drinking from a holy well, but he never returned to Camelot. My aunt Morgan le Fay made sure of that. She took the form of a beautiful young girl, and met Merlin in the forest, and enticed him to reveal to her the dark secrets of his art. And when he had laid all bare to her, she used his own spells to imprison his spirit in a hawthorn tree. Some say they have heard him calling to them in wild places, but none has ever seen his form again.

Arthur paid dearly for Merlin's madness. He had none by him to counsel caution in the wildness of his victory at Bedgrayne; none to whisper a warning when a dark beauty entered his tent that night, and offered her body for another sort of battle. That woman was my mother, Morgause, and the fruit of that night was my half-brother, Mordred. And when Mordred suckled at our mother's breast, he drew out a poison that will kill his father, Arthur. I don't need to be Merlin to foresee that.

But the battle of Bedgrayne brought Arthur good as well as ill. He not only crushed his enemies, but by his courage and nobility turned many of them into friends. My cousin Owain and I both fought against Arthur that day, but for him ever afterwards; and all my brothers followed me: Agravaine, Gaheris, gentle Gareth, and at last, Mordred.

It was Mordred's arrival at court that turned Arthur's luck against him. Mordred is weak himself; he has always known how to play on weakness in others. He made a tool of my brother Agravaine, a tool to destroy all our mother had taught him to hate, and I had learned to love. I cannot talk about it today, boy. The time will come.

But you should know, another king sent his son that day to swell King Arthur's court: King Ban, who had fought so well on Arthur's side, sent his son Lancelot. And a king with no sons sent his daughter, to be King Arthur's bride. Her name was Guinevere.

III

Sir Owain and the Lady of the Fountain

It's a grey morning, boy. It was a morning such as this when I first came to King Arthur's court, at Camelot. And as I arrived at the castle, the greyness lifted and the sun shone on the stones like the first morning of the world.

I don't think anyone can know now how it felt to join that company in the springtime of its strength. To go to the Round Table and find a chair on which Merlin had set my name in magic letters of gold; to sit amongst the foremost knights of the world, and hear them talk of battles, and rescues, and wonders. And yet there was none of the brutal, coarse talk I'd heard among my father King Lot's soldiery. No one gloated over his enemies. If they defeated a man in fair fight they asked him to come and serve King Arthur; and sometimes that man would find when he came to Camelot *his* name in gold on a chair at the table. Merlin foresaw it all.

To uphold the right. That's what we promised. To protect the weak, to help the poor, to show pity and

15

mercy to our enemies. Our strength was always to be used for others' benefit, not our own. And we felt so strong in our hearts. We thought we could save the world. Just by upholding the right. And it worked, for a little while, till we lost our way. While there were still giants to kill, and maidens to rescue, and tyrants to vanquish, it worked. But now... Who's to say what's right now? We're all in the wrong, and we can't get out of it.

The dream withered. But we made it real, for a while. I hold on to that, now everything else has gone.

It was Mordred showed us it was all a sham. When Mordred came to court. He was just the type we'd fought all those years ago: sly, and vicious, with a coward's bullying ways. He would mouth our promises, and from his lips the words seemed to edge themselves with deceit. "To uphold the right" sounded like a threat. And yet the king took him in, and favoured him, while we saw from the start that our dream was soured. We swore to protect the weak, but forgot to include ourselves. King Arthur was weak as a kitten to my mother's will after the battle of Bedgrayne. He slept with his sister, boy. He didn't know it, but he did. Mordred is his punishment. We can't escape the consequences of what we do. We can't escape.

This world is full of sadness, boy. You'll learn that soon enough. But on that morning, that grey morning riding into Camelot, when the sun broke on the castle walls, I didn't feel the sadness then. My blood tingled in my body as if it was on fire. Just to breathe the air in that castle was to be drunk with the pleasure of being alive. Each night we'd gather to drink and eat and talk. It was a story for a story, well into the night. Oh, the tales we told, boasting about our travels, "over hills, dales and lofty mountains, far further than I can tell you tonight, or tomorrow night, or any other night in this new year". That's what we used to say, when we youngsters crowed about the adventures we'd had, or would like to have had, or planned to have one day. As if the adventures don't come soon enough of their own accord. But it was all harmless, and exciting, and knowing the others were waiting to hear about them helped us when the adventures really came.

Of course not all the knights were cocky striplings like me and my cousin Owain, who came to Camelot with me. There was one, Cynan, an old fellow; there was scarcely an inch of his body unscarred, or so they said – I never saw it. One night, when we'd all said our piece, Cynan got up, and told us of an adventure that befell him, when he was young and unafraid. He was the pride of the country as a young man. He overcame dragons, giants and enchanters. He wrestled all comers at village fairs. No man could defeat him, and there was no adventure he would not undertake.

One day, Cynan was riding in search of adventure when he reached a great forest. Inside the forest was a clearing the size of a field, with a mound in the middle, and on the mound a man the size of two men of this world, carrying a great club of iron. He was a one-eyed, ill-tempered, fearsome looking wretch, and at his feet there was a stag. He greeted Cynan, and his voice was low and rumbling like the grinding together of great rocks. It seemed the ground itself was speaking. "I am the herdsman of the forest," he said. Cynan thought the fellow was simple, and laughed. "What do you herd," he asked, "here in the middle of nowhere?" The man made no answer, but took his club and struck the stag a mighty blow. Its voice belled out clear through the forest air.

Cynan heard a rustling behind him, and felt the breath of a huge lion hot upon his neck. Soon the whole clearing was filled with animals: lions, wolves, deer, adders and snakes of all sorts. Every kind of wild animal was there,

17

and there was scarcely room for him to stand. The animals looked towards their master and bowed their heads to him, and did him homage as to a king. He told the animals to depart, and they obeyed him. Then he turned to Cynan, and said, "Do not smile at me again, little man. For you see my power."

Then the herdsman of the forest asked Cynan what he sought, and when Cynan told him he was looking for adventure, told him to follow the path he was on. "When you come to a hill, climb it. From the top you will see a valley, and in the middle of the valley a huge tree. The tips of the branches of that tree are the purest green on this earth, and under the tree is a fountain, which bubbles as if it is boiling, though it is icy to the touch, and beside the fountain is a marble slab. A bowl is tied to the slab by a silver chain.

"If you truly want an adventure, you only have to fill the bowl with water from the fountain, and pour the water onto the marble slab. Then the skies will open. Thunder and lightning will fury over your head. If you bear the rain, there will come hailstones to tear your flesh. If you bear the hailstones, the sky will clear. There will not be left on the tree one single leaf. A flight of birds will settle on its branches and sing to you, and at the highest point of their song, a knight shall come. He will be riding a black horse, the purest black on this earth, and he will wear a robe of black silk over his armour and carry a spear with a black point. He will attack you, and if you flee him he will kill you. If you stay and fight on horseback, he may spare you once he has you at his mercy. If you do not call *that* an adventure, you will never have one."

So Cynan took the path the herdsman pointed out, and found the tree, and poured water from the fountain onto the marble slab. In the storm that followed it seemed as if the sky was trying to tear the earth apart. The hailstones that followed the rain stopped not at cloth, nor hair, nor skin, but only at bone. Had Cynan not had on his armour, and his shield to cover himself and his horse, they could never have survived it.

And when the storm stopped, as the herdsman predicted there was not a leaf left on the tree. To its bare branches came a flight of birds, and their song was a wonder and a joy. No two birds sang the same note, and listening to their harmonies Cynan forgot his sores where the hail had whipped him. At the peak of their song, the knight in black arrived.

"What is your meaning," shouted the knight, "that you bring such destruction to my kingdom? In all this valley there is no beast, on two legs or four, that was caught outdoors that survived the blast of that storm, save you and your horse."

Cynan gave him no answer, but made ready to fight. The two knights charged each other with all their strength. In that fight, Cynan fought as he had never fought before. Such blows, such parries, such feints, such horsemanship! Yet soon enough he was sprawled on the ground, and the black knight had his horse, and he was left with only the mud for company.

Cynan would not tell us, but we could guess his shame as he limped back on foot past the giant herdsman and mocking words followed him on his way. "In all the years since this adventure, I have spoken of it to no one," he said, "and I have heard none speak of it. Yet the place is but three days' journey from this court."

And Owain, my cousin, in the eagerness of youth, said, "Shall we not ride and see if this is still the custom of that valley, and if so seek out the adventure?" But Sir Kay spoke slightingly to him: "Your mouth does better work than your hands, Owain." All the knights laughed – I did so myself, for Kay had a cutting tongue, and those who did not wish to be lashed by it had to encourage it. And that was that. Except next morning, Owain was nowhere to be found. Sir Kay's sneer had stung him, and he had gone on his own in search of the valley of the fountain.

After three days, Owain did come upon the giant herdsman, and everything happened to him as it had to Cynan. When he arrived at the fountain, he poured water on the marble slab and, like Cynan, endured the storm with the help of his armour and his shield. Then the sky lightened, and the birds came. As their voices blended in the most perfect of all songs, the black knight arrived.

The two knights fought fiercely for half an hour, until Owain struck a blow with his sword that cut through the black knight's armour as if it were paper. When he felt this blow, the black knight turned his horse and fled, with Owain chasing after him. Though the black knight was wounded to death, his horse was fast and untired, and Owain could not catch up.

Soon they reached a great walled castle, its roofs glittering in the dying sun. As the black knight entered the castle a gate dropped down, separating him from his pursuer. Too late, Owain turned around to see another gate descending to make him prisoner. He was trapped and in his enemy's hands. So severe was the knight's wound, however, that Owain felt sure that he was safe for the time being.

When all was dark, a maiden came to the inner gate. Her clothes were silver, and she shimmered like the moon. "I beg you," said Owain, "release me from this prison."

"What I can do for you, I will," she answered, and she handed him a ring. "Put on this ring. If you turn its stone towards the palm of your hand you will be invisible to all. When they come to kill you, slip past them. I will be waiting outside, and if you put your hand on my

shoulder, I will guide you to safety. My name is Luned."
Then she left him: alone, but in better spirits than before.

Soon a party of heavily armed men came to the inner
gate, and opened it. They searched every crevice of every
wall for a sign of Owain, but he had crept out invisible,
and left them to it. While they muttered to themselves,
and crossed themselves for fear of enchantment, Owain
followed the maiden to a room safe at the top of the
castle. The room was richly decorated and furnished;
Owain had never seen anywhere so comfortable. There
he rested till the next day, when he awoke to the sound
of wailing in the castle, and knew that the black knight
was dead.

Then there was a great sound of trumpets and chanting,
and when Owain looked out of the window he saw the
black knight being carried to his grave. Of the men
carrying his coffin there was not one lower in rank than
a baron. Behind the coffin walked a lady, wild with grief,
and as she walked she wrung her hands and tore her hair.
Dishevelled as she was, she seemed to Owain the most
beautiful woman he had ever seen. Her hair was golden
like the sun. Owain asked Luned who she was. "She is
my mistress, the lady of the fountain, wife of the black
knight whom you have killed."

As he looked on the lady, Owain felt the pang of love
at his heart, as if a spear had pierced him. But a spear
wound, boy, can be salved, as you salve mine. The wound
of love can never heal. The lady could have taken no more
lasting revenge for the death of her husband. Owain knew
now that if he could not persuade her to love him in
return, the rest of his life would be empty of meaning.
Luned saw this too, and was sad, for she loved Owain
herself. That was why she rescued him. But she loved
him so well she decided to help him even in this. "Wait
here, while I go wooing for you," she said.

22

Luned then went to her mistress and asked her why she was crying and lamenting for the death of the black knight. "It would be far better if you set yourself to find another champion."

"That I could never do," sighed the lady.

"You could," said Luned, "if you found another man as good as the black knight, or even better."

At this the lady wept again. She called Luned a monster, and disloyal, and hard-hearted, but allowed her to continue speaking.

"Your lands must be defended," Luned told her. "Unless you find a new knight to protect the fountain, all that you have will be taken from you. Only a knight of King Arthur's court could help you. I will go there to seek your new husband."

Luned pretended to set off for Camelot, but really she just stayed hidden with Owain in the upper room for six days. Then she went again to the lady. "I have been to King Arthur's court, mistress, and have brought back a knight."

"Bring him to me tomorrow at noon," said the lady, "and I will see him."

The next day Owain dressed in rich robes and went with Luned to see the lady. When she saw him, she turned to Luned and said, "This man has not the look of a traveller."

"And what of that?" asked Luned.

"By the night stars, I believe this is the man who killed my husband."

"And if he did, lady, all the better for you. For he proved the worthier."

So the lady took my cousin Owain as her husband. He became the knight of the fountain, and kept it secure by the strength of his right arm.

We at Camelot knew nothing of this. But when three years had passed, and no news had come of Owain, we set out with Cynan as our guide to seek the valley of the fountain, a whole troop of knights with King Arthur at our head.

Kay was not a bad man, though he mocked the young knights, and called my brother Gareth "Pretty Hands". He just had a bitter tongue. He knew that it was his taunt that had sent Owain to that valley, and for all we knew to his death, and he felt guilty. So when we reached the tree and the fountain, Sir Kay begged to be the first challenger. Before anyone could deny him, he dashed the water on the stone. After the storm had passed and the birds had sung, a knight in black appeared, and gave him a thrashing. I remember, Kay never liked being beaten; he claimed the birds' singing had distracted him, or otherwise he would never have taken such a fall. But I doubt it, for the black knight served every member of our company the same, until only the king and I had not yet challenged him.

So I in my turn spilled the icy water of the fountain, drop by drop on the marble slab. The storm that followed brought us to our knees with its fury; yet it passed, and when it passed, there were the birds, and the black knight as before.

I have been in many fights, but rarely such a desperate battle as that. That black knight seemed to have the strength of ten. But he was weakened, no doubt, by his bouts with Sir Kay and the others, and though I could not defeat him, he could not unhorse me. Not till we both fell exhausted to the ground. We couldn't move. The visor of my helmet fell open, and the black knight shouted "Gawain! Gawain!" and I heard my cousin Owain. I'd fought him many a time in play, but never before in such deadly earnest. We were so happy to see each other, we couldn't do anything else but quarrel about who had won the fight. He gave the prize to me, and I to him. At last the king settled it. "Neither of you proved the stronger," he said.

Owain was delighted to see us. He told the king, "I have been preparing a feast for you for three years. I knew that you would come to seek me." He took us to the castle, and we ate and drank every kind of good thing till we could eat and drink no more. That was an enchanted place! In the valley of the fountain, a man could truly find his heart's desire.

But to have your heart's desire and to live content with it are two different things, and Owain felt restless in his valley. So the lady of the fountain gave him leave to travel back to Camelot with the king, and stay with his old friends for three months. But I heard her tell him, "The ring that Luned gave you to make you invisible has another power. If a true lover wears it, he will suffer no harm or misfortune, so long as he remembers his love. But if he should forget, then he is no longer worthy of the ring, and though his path was plain when he rode from this valley, it shall be twisted and tangled when he rides back."

Owain laughed at the suggestion that he might forget her. But once back at Camelot the memory of his enchanted valley seemed to slip from his mind like a dream. He stayed three years, not three months. At the end of that time, Luned arrived at the court one day without warning, and seized the ring from Owain's hand. Only then did he remember what he had lost.

Owain set off the next day, but search as he might he could not find the way to the valley of the fountain. He despaired of ever seeing the lady or Luned again, and wandered wild in the mountains, never washing, never resting, never eating, till his beard was long and his face was black and his clothes were all in tatters.

One day, Owain came upon a great castle. He made his way to the gate, and there he collapsed. As he lay there,

25

the countess whose castle it was saw him, as she was walking with her maid. She sent the maid back to the castle to fetch a jar she kept by her bed. When the maid brought it, she told her, "This jar contains a precious ointment. Though it is worth more than all my possessions, and it seems a waste to use it on an old tramp, yet I cannot let this man die. I will rub it on his heart, and the life will come back into him."

When the ointment touched him, Owain rose up as healthy as he had ever been, though he still looked filthy and ragged. The countess took him back to the castle, where he bathed and put on new clothes, and the countess saw that he was a handsome young man, and not a tramp at all.

Soon afterwards, the countess' castle was attacked by an evil earl, who had already seized all her lands and who now wanted her castle for himself. The countess was a widow, and had no knights to defend her. When Owain saw the earl's army, he asked if his hostess had a horse and armour he could borrow. She showed him the stables and the armoury. "Take what you want," she said, with a break in her voice. "They will all be the earl's by tomorrow." So Owain chose the finest stallion in the stables, and armour and arms fit for a king. Then he asked which man was the earl, and the countess pointed him out.

Owain rode straight through the earl's army, scattering men to either side, till he reached the earl himself. Owain pulled him from the saddle, and rode back to the castle dragging the earl behind him. He said to the countess, "Here is my present to you, in return for the ointment you gave me."

To save his own life the earl gave the countess back all her lands, and to win his freedom he gave her half of his own lands, and a great store of gold and jewels.

After that Owain left the countess, and went off once more in search of the valley of the fountain.

One day, as he rode through a forest, Owain heard a tremendous commotion, and hurrying towards the noise he saw a great roaring lion and a writhing green snake fighting a dancing battle in the middle of a clearing. When the lion attacked, the snake slithered aside, and when the lion retreated, the snake weaved and struck, uncoiling its body with the speed of the wind. It was all the lion could do to keep its feet, and its strength was failing. Owain had sworn, like us all, to protect the weak, and though he had never thought of lions as needing his help, he didn't waste a moment, but drew his sword and cut the serpent in two.

Afterwards, as Owain rode on his way, the lion padded by his side, more like a pet cat than a wild beast. But if anyone came near them, the lion roared and bared its teeth, and always after that time it fought at Owain's side. He became one of the most feared knights in Britain, and people called him the Knight of the Lion.

And that's all I know of Owain, boy. Folk say the lion led him back at last to the valley of the fountain, and its lady. I don't know. I hope so... I never saw him again.

I could wish I'd had Owain's fate. To be lord of an enchanted valley, and live there safe from the world, safe from this grief that has come upon us. But that was not my fate, and in those days I did not wish it so. I pitied him, rather, and gloried in the world. Those were fine days, fine days. We were the fairest fellowship of noble knights that ever served a Christian king.

IV

Sir Gawain and the Green Knight

Another foul morning, boy, and Lancelot still skulking in his castle.

I told you yesterday of my cousin Owain, and his adventures in the valley of the fountain. While Owain was languishing at court, forgetting his lady, I was getting myself in a tangle with a lady too. You'll have noticed some of the older knights wearing a green belt? That's in honour of me, they'll say, if you ask them the reason for it. Here's how it was.

It was Christmas time. All the knights who could manage it came back to Camelot at that time, for fifteen days of feasting and storytelling. Each evening King Arthur would call for a tale, of adventure, or romance, or of some marvel, before the company sat down to eat.

On New Year's Day we got more than just a tale. I remember it so clearly. The hall was full of noise as always, and then, suddenly, dead silence. No one was speaking, no one was moving. And into the hall, into the silence rode the largest man I ever saw, on a huge warhorse. He was dressed all in green. And, by God, his skin was green, and his hair was green; he was bright green from head to foot. In one hand he held a bunch of green holly, and in the other an axe, gleaming and razor-sharp, with a blade of green and gold. Only his eyes flashed red like holly berries.

That terrible green knight just sat on his horse, and looked each man in the eye. Each man looked away. You felt he saw right inside you. At last he spoke. "Where's the ruler of this rabble?" he jeered. "The brave King Arthur."

Arthur stood forward. "I am Arthur," he said. "I bid you welcome, if you come in peace. If not, you will find many here ready to meet you in combat."

"I don't fight with beardless boys," said the intruder. "It is not combat I want, but a game." He stroked his axe and smiled. "I wonder if there is anyone here brave enough to trade me blow for blow with this axe of mine. I will suffer the first stroke, and he must then take the second from me within a year and a day, if I survive."

Of course the king offered at once to satisfy the stranger. "Your game is foolish," he said, "but if you wish to play it, so be it. Give me the axe." But my blood was hot within me, for shame of looking away when the green knight held my eyes, and I would not let the king meddle with such a ruffian. I claimed the adventure for my own.

King Arthur let me take the axe. "Strike hard, nephew," he said. "Strike hard enough, and you will be able to bear any blow he gives you in return." He tried to make a joke of it, but even his voice was thin with fear.

The green knight dismounted, bent forward, and bared his neck to my axe. I set my left foot firmly on the ground, raised the axe, and swung it down. The green knight's head rolled away across the floor, and red blood burst from his body, bright against the green.

The monstrous knight never faltered. He walked towards the table and picked up his head. Once back in the saddle, he held up the head, and the lips moved. He said, "Gawain: keep your promise. In a year and a day meet me at the Green Chapel, where I shall return your stroke. Come, or let all men call you coward." And then he left, as suddenly as he had come.

"Let us eat," said King Arthur, "for now we have truly seen a marvel." I still stood in the hall, the axe hanging useless in my hand. The king called to me, "Gawain, hang up your axe. You have hewn enough." I took my place at the table. The food was served, and a hubbub of talking and eating filled the space where the green knight's silence had been. But I did not talk or eat again that night.

The year passed as those before had done: spring melted into summer, and summer into autumn. As winter drew near, I prepared myself for my journey to the Green Chapel, and, as best I could, for the journey which surely lay beyond that. I was shriven of my sins, and I painted on my shield the five-pointed star of the pentangle, which is also called the endless knot, the emblem of perfect truth.

One day, when the brittle winter light made the solid stone of Camelot as fragile as a dream, I mounted my horse Gringalet and took my leave. For many miles I felt the keen gaze of the king follow me on my way.

At last I was out of sight or help of any friend. I travelled through wild country on that journey. Often I found nowhere to stay and nothing to eat; I found robbers, wild beasts, and evil creatures I will not name. Always I asked those I met for directions to the Green Chapel, but no one I met had ever heard of such a place.

That was a bad winter, boy, worse than this. More nights than I wished I slept among bare rocks, in my armour, shivering, wet and cold.

By Christmas Day I had still not met anyone who knew of the green knight or his chapel, and my spirits were low. I rode with my head down. Even the song of the birds on the branches above seemed melancholy that day. I prayed to God I might come to some shelter in which to celebrate Christmas. And when I looked up, there in answer was a mighty castle in the distance, shadowed like a papercut against the sky. I spurred Gringalet on.

I was met in the castle courtyard by a burly, brown-bearded man who clasped my hands as I dismounted. "Welcome, sir knight," he said. "My castle is yours, while you choose to stay." His face was as threatening as fire, but his words were noble.

I was led to a chamber and dressed in soft rich robes. I was warm and happy for the first time since leaving Camelot. For the first evening in many a long day, I enjoyed wine and talk and warmth, instead of rain water, my own thoughts, and the winter's cold. My host, Sir Bertilak, was hospitality itself, and his wife: well, she took my breath away. She was as fresh and as beautiful as the crescent moon. But there was an old woman with her that I didn't take to, an old crone, dressed in black like the moon's dark side.

For three days we lived in high style, with feasting, and dancing, and music. And I'll tell you straight that the more we talked, and the more we laughed, the more I fell for Sir Bertilak's lady.

Finally, it was time to go. Sir Bertilak wanted me to stay on, but I told him I must seek the Green Chapel, to keep my appointment with the monstrous green knight. Imagine my surprise when Sir Bertilak told me that the Green Chapel was not two miles from his castle. This meant I could stay for three more days with him. He said, "You still need rest after your hard journey. Sleep late tomorrow, and my wife shall come to keep you company when you wake. I shall rise early, and go hunting. We will play a game: whatever I win in the hunt, I will give to you; whatever you win at home is mine in return.

The three days that followed are the centre of my life, boy. Everything led to them, or from them. Yet I can't now separate what I did and saw from what I thought and dreamed. Perhaps I couldn't even then. Each day, as we'd agreed, Sir Bertilak went hunting, and I stayed behind to rest and refresh myself for my ordeal in the Green Chapel. But it seemed to me that part of me went with Sir Bertilak also. I knew his movements as closely, as intimately as I hear Sir Lancelot's breathing now. I felt them at the roots of my heart.

So when I awoke on the first morning, I could trace in the dappling of the sunlight on the wall of my chamber, the deer fleeing from the hounds, into the dales, or onto high ground. I could hear in the soughing of the wind the notes of the bugle that urged the hounds on. I could feel in the movement of my blood the wild joy with which Sir Bertilak pursued his quarry.

And when Sir Bertilak's lady entered the room, my heart leapt within me like a deer. The rustle of her gown made my bones ache.

It seemed, boy, that one moment she was at the door; the next, at my side. I was afraid of her, and of myself. As we talked, she tangled me in double meanings like a deer in a thicket. I could not escape her. And yet I remembered my host. How could I not, when I felt in the air each arrow shiver from his bow, and heard in the space between my ear and brain the cries of the does as they fell.

All my nerves were outside my skin. She was no nearer me than you are now, but I felt her pressing close, so close that when she moved it was almost a pain to me. And at last I reached across the space between us, and as the hounds dragged down a doe I pulled her to me, and took a kiss like a bruise on my heart.

When Sir Bertilak returned, he gave me the prize of his hunt. And I seized him in my arms, and kissed the roughness of his beard.

Next day, I swore not to give way. If I must die, I wanted no new stain of dishonour on my soul. Yet I could think of nothing else but Sir Bertilak's lady. She haunted my sleep and my waking. I was barely aware that morning who I was or where I was, when she entered and kissed me, so sweetly, so sweetly: her lips tasted of pears. I tried to talk of war, and honour, and the duties of a knight, but she would talk of nothing but love, and said the whole duty of a knight was to win the heart of each lady he admired.

The moving shadows on my wall showed me that up in the hills Sir Bertilak hunted an enormous old boar, grim and stubborn. He cornered it beneath a gaunt crag, but it burst through the hounds, tossing them aside. The hunters hallooed, and urged the dogs on. Again and again the boar turned and fought, till the dogs yelped and the nobles cowered in fear. But at last in a rushing stream Sir Bertilak plunged his sword deep into its body; the dogs did the rest.

And in my room I turned from the lady again and again, till her tears flowed, and I took her once more in my arms and kissed her.

Sir Bertilak when he returned was full of the chase. He gave me the head of the boar he had slain. "Now," he said. "Give me what you have won." So I embraced him once more, and kissed him once, twice on the lips. He roared with laughter. I felt his laughter seared through me, exposing every shameful thought and deed of my life. I told him I must leave next day. He would have none of it. "There's no need to go yet," he said. "Anyway, our bargain still has a day to run. I've had the worst of it so far, but, as they say, third time pays for all."

That night I dreamed of Sir Bertilak holding the boar's head high, and then of the green knight holding aloft his gory head. I woke from this vision to find the lady by my side, her lips on mine. She wore a loose robe of white silk, bound at the waist with a green sash threaded with gold. She leaned forward and kissed me again, but I pushed her away. She looked straight into my eyes, and I felt my soul twist into hers on the thread of our gaze. To look away, to cut that thread, took all my strength. And then she cried again. "You love some other woman more than me," she said.

"I have no love," I told her, "and want none."

"That is the worst answer of all," she said. "Kiss me once more and I will go." So we kissed; and that kiss tasted rank with pain.

Across his estates, Sir Bertilak hunted the wily fox. It doubled back, hid, concealed its scent, and led him through every bush and briar on his land.

The lady hesitated at my door. "I wish," she said.

"What?" I asked.

"I wish I had something of yours - even just a glove - to remember you by."

"I brought no precious things with me on this journey," I told her. "For we are told we can take nothing with us from this world. I travelled hard and light, with no trinkets in my baggage. You have deserved more than I can give; I would not demean you with a glove."

She said, "If you will give me nothing of yours, at least accept this from me." She held out a ring of red gold set with a sparkling green stone; even Guinevere had none so fine. I told her I would take no gift, for I had nothing

35

for her. She said, "If you will not take the ring, at least take this sash for a keepsake."

"I will be your servant through fire and ice," I said, "but I will accept no gift."

"This sash looks a simple thing," she urged, "but it has a hidden power. Whoever wears it cannot be harmed. No one need know you wear it. When I entered, you were moaning in your dream. Would you not sleep sounder tonight with this wrapped round you; will you not fare better tomorrow?"

I had thought, boy, I could face out all temptation. Perhaps we never really know ourselves until the last extreme. I took the sash.

As soon as Sir Bertilak came home, weary, scratched and miserable from the chase, I kissed him three times, but I kept back the sash.

"I have nothing for you but this evil-smelling fox's skin," he said.

Next morning was a sad leave-taking. The weather threatened ill. Clouds covered the sky; snow snittered to the ground; the wind moaned. But under my red surcoat I wore the green sash, and that kept me warmer than any clothes.

The way was hard. A heavy, choking mist was everywhere. I tell you freely, despite the sash I was tempted just to ride on my way, let folk think what they will. But I thought of the trust King Arthur placed in me, and I turned my horse into the valley of the Green Chapel.

At first I could see no chapel: only an old barrow like a fairy hill, beside a fast-running stream. The mound was hollow, and open at the end. It was all overgrown with grass. It looked a devilish place; I thought it must have been the Devil himself had lured me there.

Suddenly from within the mound I heard a terrible noise. It was as if a scythe was being sharpened on a grindstone, but the noise was as loud as the thunder of water in a mill. It seemed as if the rocks would split apart with it, and my head with them.

I called out, "Who's there?", and the green knight sprang out from the opening, whirling a battle-axe. His body, his beard, his hair and his clothes were the same violent, unnatural green as before.

"Welcome, Sir Gawain," he said. "You have kept your word. Last year you struck off my head. Now it is my turn. Take off your helmet and stretch out your neck."

I uncovered my neck, and knelt down before him. He lifted his axe, and swung it down. I felt it parting the air as it fell towards me, and flinched. He stopped the blow. "You are not Gawain," he sneered, "shrinking from the axe like a servant cringing from his master's whip."

"I'll not do so again," I assured him.

He lifted the axe again, and brought it slicing down. Yet though I kept as still as stone, he stopped the blow once more, just before the blade reached my neck.

I felt my temper rise. "Do not play with me," I shouted. "Strike, if you are going to." He raised the axe for the third time.

The blade cut straight and true through the air; but again he checked the blow. This time, though, the axe nicked my flesh. When I saw my blood dripping to the snow, I leapt aside and drew my sword. "You have had your stroke. Now, let us fight."

But the green knight just leaned on the handle of his axe. "Put away your sword, Sir Gawain," he said. "I do not wish you ill. I promised you a blow, and I have given it. The game is over."

"I am Sir Bertilak," he told me. "The old lady at the castle was your aunt, Morgan le Fay, who gave me this shape by witchcraft, to try the courage and honour of King Arthur's knights. I sent my wife to test you. For

37

two days you kissed my wife and gave the kisses back to me. Two times I lifted my axe and did not strike. On the third day you gave me the kisses but you kept back the sash. You thought it would save you from harm, trusting more in magic than in God. Therefore I gave you that wound."

I was so ashamed I could not speak. I have worn that sash both night and day ever since, as a token of my failure in truth to man and trust in God. See, here, about my waist. But all the other knights of our fellowship, when they heard the story, swore to wear a green sash too; to share in my defeat: though they called it a victory.

It's a strange thought: no doubt Sir Lancelot is wearing just such a sash, even as we speak.

V

The Marriage of of Sir Gawain

I expect, boy, you think you'll make your life: hammer it to the shape you want as a blacksmith hammers metal. But life makes us, not the other way round. I can see that clearly now, as I tell you, as I tell myself the stories that have brought me to this tent. Why, even the king has had to live on the terms life offered to him; he hasn't made his own.

I'll tell you a story, to show you how life takes us, and shakes us, and makes us do its bidding.

The king was travelling one time in the north of his realm, when his path was blocked by a huge hairy man holding a wooden club. "Out of my way and let me pass," said the king.

"Pass if you can," said the huge hairy man.

I'll teach this lout a lesson, thought the king. Up went his sword; down came the club. And somehow the king of England was lying in the dirt, learning a lesson himself. The huge hairy man beat King Arthur black and blue, and then tied the king's hands and feet beneath the belly of his horse and led him away.

Next morning, King Arthur woke where he had been thrown down, in a corner of the great hall in his captor's house. The huge hairy man was poking him with a stick. "Still alive, eh?" said the man. He drew a wicked greasy knife from his belt and cut the king's bonds. Arthur tried to stretch. He was as stiff as an old horse.

"You're my boot boy now," said the huge hairy man. "You do what I say."

So for weeks the king was a drudge, fetching and carrying for this surly, bullying master. At last he could bear his life no longer. There was no escape. So he humbled himself and knelt, though a king kneels to no man, and begged for release from his hard service. "If you will not accept a ransom," he said, "tell me what it is you do want of me. If it is in my power, you shall have it. But let me go."

The huge hairy man laughed his slow rumbling laugh, a laugh that was more than half a snarl, and said, "I will let you go, *king*, on one condition. Within a year and a day you will bring me the answer to a riddle I shall ask you. If you bring no answer, you must answer with your life."

King Arthur did not know what riddle he would be asked, but he was good at riddling. Such games were popular at court. So he eagerly accepted the terms. "Now tell me," he said. "What is the riddle I must answer?"

"Simply this," replied the huge hairy man. "You must tell me what it is that women most desire."

"In a year and a day, then," said the king.

Riding back to court, King Arthur asked everyone he met what it was that women most desired. Some said "a good husband", and some "a rich one"; some said "handsome sons", and some "beautiful daughters";

some said "clothes" or "jewels"; some "flattery", or "attention"; many a husband said "a life of idleness". But never did the king get an answer that he thought would satisfy the huge hairy man.

No one at court could tell him the answer either. He asked me for my help, and he rode east and I rode west, asking, questioning. At last we had both filled a whole book with answers, but never a one with which all agreed.

When King Arthur set out to fulfil his promise, he took the two books of answers with him, but he was too discouraged now to ask any more people the question that had seemed so easy a year ago. He rode silent and alone through the dark and gloomy woods.

On one narrow winding path his horse stumbled. Looking up, King Arthur saw a clearing filled with light, and four and twenty of the folk it is better not to name dancing there. He urged his horse forward; the dancers disappeared. Now there was only a dark loathly womanish figure, draped in black, sitting on a rock in the middle of the clearing. So ugly, so old and so evil it looked that Arthur shuddered, and turned his horse aside.

A cry that was more like a croak stopped him. The figure rose, and spoke. Arthur could see that it was indeed a haglike old woman. He rode towards her to hear what she had to say to him. As he approached, mist coiled and wreathed round the legs of his horse.

"King Arthur is your name," the woman said, "and you ride to your doom if you do not answer the hardest question ever asked. Speak, if this is true."

"It is true, though how you know it I cannot guess."

"What is it, then, King Arthur, that women most desire?" the hag demanded.

Arthur racked his brains once again, searching for an answer that was true for every woman, and once again he failed. "I cannot tell you," he said.

41

"But I can tell you," replied the withered woman, "if you will grant my wish."

"It is granted," said Arthur without thought. "Now, tell me the answer to the riddle." The crone whispered her answer in his ear, and Arthur, seeing at once that it was the true one, breathed a sigh of relief from the depths of his heart. "And now, good lady," he said, "what is your wish of me? Gold, jewels, titles, lands – all these are yours for the asking."

"I want no gold, or jewels, or titles, or lands," she answered, "but simply this: that in one month's time when I come to your court you will marry me to one of your knights."

King Arthur's reply died in his throat. None of his knights would wish to marry such a bride. Before he could speak, she had faded into the mist and he was alone.

When King Arthur arrived at the house where he had been a servant and knelt to a master, he did not know what to do. He tried every answer that he and I had collected, but each time the huge hairy man just laughed and shook his head. At last, Arthur ran out of answers and fell silent. He would rather die than give the old woman's solution and condemn one of his knights to marriage with such a creature.

"So you have not been able to find the answer. In that case, I shall have your head." The giant roared with laughter. "Your famous knights are obviously as puny in the brain as they are in the arm."

King Arthur couldn't help himself. He fixed his taunter with his eyes, and slowly, deliberately he recited,

"Since Eve first walked, her one desire is still
In all her dealings, just to have her will."

He turned and rode away, and the huge hairy man made no attempt to stop him.

When King Arthur arrived home and told his story, in all the court there was no woman - girl, wife or widow - who would gainsay the old hag's answer. We all rejoiced that the king was safe. Only Arthur did not smile. He told us that to get the answer he had promised the old woman the hand of one of his knights in marriage. "And," he said, "she is the foulest-looking woman I ever saw."

I had been ensnared by beauty in Sir Bertilak's castle; I knew that the pleasure we take in another's face is mostly the reflection of our own vanity. This woman sounded like a fit companion for my days and nights of shame. I told the king I would gladly wed her and wed her again, though she were a fiend and foul as Beelzebub. So the wedding date was set, and preparations for the feast set in hand.

At last the day came, and all the court lined the streets to welcome the old woman who had saved the king. My bride-to-be rode into Camelot on a moth-eaten broken-down old donkey, and the crowd recoiled in horror from her. From her filthy tangled hair, bald in patches so her scaly scalp showed through, to her claw-like feet, there was no limb or feature that was not deformed and ugly. Her shapeless scrawny body was bad enough, but it was her face that made the onlookers shudder: her skin was coarse and wrinkled, her eyes bleared, her nose dribbling and warty, her mouth a simple gash, with shrunken lips drawn back over yellow, decaying teeth. Dressed in a white lace gown, she seemed a horrid mockery of a bride.

It was, in truth, a dismal ceremony. And at the wedding feast, while all around her toyed with their food, my bride ignored both plates and cutlery. With her ragged nails she tore into the bread and meat, cramming food into her mouth till the gravy ran down her chin. She ate enough for six, and drank enough for nine.

When we were left alone in the bridal chamber, I could not control the trembling of my hands. The blood had drained from my face. The hideous woman plucked at my arm. "What's the matter, chuck?" she asked. "Come on, give us a kiss."

My gorge rose. But I swear, as I turned to kiss her, I was overtaken with such a loving pity for her, that people should spurn her like some vile animal, that her touch no longer revolted me, ugly as she was. I closed my eyes and kissed her on her watery old mouth.

Then she embraced me, and said, "Come, look at me, husband, for we two now are one." And I opened my eyes.

There she stood, an unscarred graceful girl of no more than eighteen winters, such a beauty trembling in her I fell to my knees before it. The chamber was full of light.

"I am your bride," she said. "I was enchanted into that foul shape by my evil father, the huge hairy man who overcame King Arthur. Your kiss has freed me, but not completely. Now you have the choice of two things: you may have me in this shape either by day or by night, but not both. For twelve hours out of each twenty-four I must still appear as loathsome as I did when you married me. Think hard, Sir Gawain, before you choose. Imagine how I will feel as I walk among the ladies of the court in that witch-like shape by day; how you will feel if I greet you in that shape each night. Consider well, and choose the lesser of the two evils."

I was so overcome with her loveliness I scarcely needed to think. "It is you, my bride," I said, "on whom the main burden of this dreadful enchantment falls. You choose for both of us and I will be content. Whatever is your wish is my wish also."

She smiled, and said, "Your love has solved my father's riddle. You have given me what women most desire, my own will, and the enchantment is now completely dissolved. This will be my shape forever now, and I will be beautiful both night and day."

Yes, boy, we think we take our own decisions, but in the end they're taken for us. At least that's so for men in this world, poor creatures that we are. Even for the king. Even, though I curse him with every painful breath I draw, even for Sir Lancelot.

VI

The Fair Unknown

Tell me, boy, do you want to be a knight? I expect you do. That's why you lads come to court, and cluster round the king to seek his favour. That's why you've been lumbered with me to look after. The king probably thought, six months as squire to old Gawain and this one will be running home to mother: eh? But you're not gone yet. So I'll tell you about another lad, just about your age, who came to Camelot.

He was a country youth, an unschooled whopstraw. He refused to give any name, and because he was so fine-boned and easy in his bearing, people called him the Fair Unknown.

Now the other youths at court would pick their time to ask the king to grant their wishes: to be made a knight, or to be given lands, or to be found a wealthy bride. But the Fair Unknown kept himself to himself. He seemed content to wait for what would come to him, rather than grasping at what passed him by.

47

At last the king asked him outright what he would most like. "Only," said the Fair Unknown, "that you grant me the next adventure that comes to court."

"It shall be yours," said the king.

That very day, a maiden rode into Camelot, astride a milk-white mare. Her name was Ellen. Behind her on the mare sat a dwarf, a handsome enough fellow, but only a few feet high. His hands were on her shoulders, and he was singing a lament, or a love song, I forget which; perhaps both at the same time. His name was Theodelain.

When the dwarf came to the end of his song, Ellen raised her voice, and said, "The Lady of Sinadon is foully imprisoned. I seek a knight, King Arthur, to set her free by means of the feat of the bold kiss."

At once the Fair Unknown sprang to his feet, and claimed the quest for himself. King Arthur could not deny him, though his heart misgave him at the thought of the dangers the lad would face.

Ellen did not hide her scorn and disappointment. "What! A witless, beardless Johnny-raw? Give me a real knight, King Arthur, one of the Knights of the Round Table!"

But the king said, "I promised the next adventure to the Fair Unknown, and he shall have it."

And then, because Ellen had asked for a knight to free the Lady of Sinadon, King Arthur knighted the Fair Unknown. I armed the lad myself, while Ellen and Theodelain rode away without him in disgust.

The Fair Unknown soon caught up with them, but they ignored him, as if he were a stray dog following them in the street. If he dared to ride by Ellen's side, she made fun of him, and called him names, and suggested he would be happier back in the farmyard. The dwarf never said a word, but just sat glumly behind his mistress. At last, the Fair Unknown dropped back, and followed a little way behind, determined at all cost to free the Lady of Sinadon.

So they rode, till they came to the Castle Adventurous. Beside that castle is the Bridge of Peril, and on the bridge they met a huge and threatening knight. By his green shield, adorned with three gold coins, they knew him for Sir William of the Branch, a treacherous, ungodly man.

"If you wish to cross here," said Sir William, "you must fight me first."

The Fair Unknown replied, "Let us pass, for we have far to ride." But Sir William would not let them by.

"Better go home while you still can," sneered Ellen. "That's a real knight on that horse, not a sack of grain. He's what I call a knight: solid as an oak."

"I have seen great oaks laid low by the wind's strokes," said the Fair Unknown, and he lifted his lance from its rest.

So they fought, and at last the Fair Unknown brought Sir William to the ground by the strength of his arm. "Go now to King Arthur," he said, "and tell him you were vanquished by the Fair Unknown."

As Sir William travelled to Camelot he met three knights, his nephews, and told them of his shameful defeat at the hands of an unknown stripling in front of a maiden and a dwarf. "We will avenge you," they said, and spurred their horses to catch up with the insolent youth. But when they reached their quarry they fared no better than their uncle, and the Fair Unknown sent them back to King Arthur with the same message.

Then Ellen turned to him and asked his pardon for her cruelty, "For I see that I have won a champion indeed."

As they neared the city of Sinadon, they found themselves in thick forest far from all human dwellings. So the three made themselves a shelter for the night by cutting green branches, and Theodelain and the Fair Unknown took turns to keep a watch. At midnight, Theodelain saw a fire in the distance, and woke the others. "Danger is near," he said, "I smell roasting."

The Fair Unknown armed himself, and rode towards the fire. There he saw a grisly giant, red and foul. In one hand the giant held a screaming girl, and with the other he turned a huge spit, on which a whole boar was cooking.

The Fair Unknown rode towards the ogre, his spear in his hand. The red giant roared, and thrust the spear aside like a thorn. The giant brandished the spit above his head, with the boar still cooking on it, and gave the Fair Unknown such a blow that his horse fell dead.

The giant let the girl go, and with his free hand he tore a tree from the ground to use as a second club. It was then the Fair Unknown showed he could be cool as well as courageous in peril. When the giant raised his clubs high, the Fair Unknown leapt under his guard and stabbed upwards, piercing the ogre's heart.

When the giant fell, the earth shook with his weight.

The three took the girl they had rescued to her home, and then rode on till at last they arrived at Sinadon. Then the Fair Unknown saw why men shrank back and crossed themselves at the name, calling it the Waste City.

Sinadon's wide streets were empty and forlorn. Doors, windows and roofs gaped wide; marble pillars lay crashed and broken on the ground. Weeds pushed up through every crack and crevice, and rats and nameless creatures lurked in the shadows. Everything was hushed, but behind the silence was the whisper of fear.

At the gates, which hung listlessly off their hinges, the steward of the city, Sir Lambard, met them, and he and the Fair Unknown jousted. The Fair Unknown rocked Sir Lambard in his saddle like a child in its cradle, till the steward called "Enough!" Sir Lambard turned to Ellen and said, "I thought at first you had brought back a boy, but I see now it is a tiger."

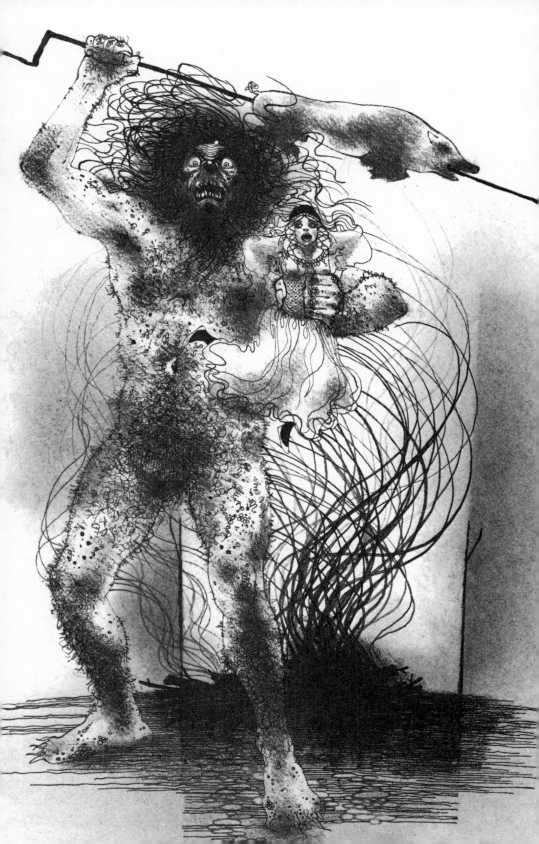

"Now," said the Fair Unknown. "Who is this knight who holds the Lady of Sinadon prisoner, and keeps the city in dread?"

"No knight," said Sir Lambard, "but a foul enchanter, named Mabon. False in flesh and bone he is, though a mortal man and no devil. He keeps our lady prisoner, and day and night torments her. We hear her cries, but we cannot help her. None but a new-made knight who does not know his own name may enter the castle, so strong is Mabon's magic."

Up spoke the Fair Unknown. "I am that knight. I do not know my name, nor ever have, nor who my father is. By God's grace I shall rescue the Lady of Sinadon."

Sir Lambard led the Fair Unknown through the deserted streets to the castle gate, and wished him luck. The Fair Unknown entered the castle, and all about him he heard music and sweet noises, though he could see no musicians. Cobwebs hung everywhere, and dust wheeled and floated in the shafts of sunlight that reached through the castle windows, fingers of light in the eerie darkness.

In the wreck of the great hall, the Fair Unknown sat down at the head of the table, and instantly the music stopped. Every door and window in the castle rattled and banged, and with a flash of lightning the roof of the hall caved in around him.

With that the sorcerer Mabon entered. He knew that no spell of his could harm the Fair Unknown, for the power of magic lies in naming, and the Fair Unknown had no name. So Mabon drew his sword, and met the new-made knight as man to man. They fought with great fury, but all Mabon's skill could not defeat the valour of the Fair Unknown. At last the lad dealt the sorcerer his death blow, with the sword I had given him when he set out from Camelot. Mabon's body seemed to crumble, and collapse in on itself, till only a little pile of ash remained, and a wisp of smoke in the air.

The Fair Unknown knelt down, to give thanks for his deliverance. As he knelt, a gap appeared in the wall to his left, and from it emerged a fearsome dragon. Its body and wings shone like burnished gold. Its tail was horrible, and its paws were grim. Most dreadful of all, its head was that of a beautiful woman. Cold pulsed through the hall.

The Fair Unknown knew that this was the Lady of Sinadon, trapped in a prison terrible beyond imagining, and he knew what he must do to free her. One kiss, and she would be freed. But he could not move. Fear coursed through his veins; sweat ran down his cheeks. He could neither advance nor run.

Then he remembered the vows he swore to King Arthur when he was made a knight, and he willed himself to move. Stumbling forward, he flung his arms around the monster's neck and kissed it full on the lips. When he opened his eyes again he was holding in his arms the fair Lady of Sinadon, naked and trembling.

"Welcome, Guinglain son of Gawain, my deliverer," she said.

Yes, boy, yes. It was my son.

Why did he not know me? That is a dark tale, and none to my credit, and I do not wish to tell it now, with evening closing in. Let this suffice: on my very first quest, in anger and haste, I killed a woman. It was an ill start to the life I had vowed to follow. And because of it this curse was laid on me, that my first-born son must be brought up alone and unaware of his parentage, and I must not greet him as a father till he had achieved some great adventure.

When he came back to court, with Ellen and Theodelain, and the Lady of Sinadon to be his bride, I could love him as a father at last. Forty days and forty nights we filled with celebration for the wedding of

Guinglain and the lady he had won by his steadfast courage.

We were still happy then. Mordred had not come.

VII

Sir Perceval

I have told you now some of the marvels of my young days, when the whole world seemed full of magic. It was as if there was an extra colour in the landscape, which isn't there now.

The world dulled when Perceval left it.

We don't talk much of Perceval, we who remain. But we think of him. For Perceval understood the great mystery of the world, the mystery of God's gift to us of life and death. Yet Perceval - I'll speak bluntly - was a fool among men.

Perceval was brought up by his mother, in the lovely wildness of Wales. His mother kept him from all knowledge of the world, and he grew up a simple, ignorant, hulking lad, dressed in skins and skilled in nothing but throwing his home-made javelins.

One day, five knights in armour rode through the forest near Perceval's home. The crash and clatter of their progress made the trees ring, and the untaught lad thought

55

the Devil was come for him. Then the riders came out of the trees, and when he saw the sunlight flashing off their polished armour he fell on his knees, crying, "These must be the shining angels my mother told me about!"

I was one of those five knights. I held my comrades back, thinking the lad was touched in the head and afraid, and rode forward alone. "Do not be afraid," I said.

"I was not," said he. He looked at me with round innocent eyes, and asked me, "Are you God?"

"No, in faith!"

"Then are you an angel?"

"I am a knight."

"I never met a knight before," the boy said, "or heard of one: but I wish I could be one."

I asked him where we were, for to tell the truth we were lost. He paid me no attention. His eye had been caught by my lance. "What's this?" he asked.

"A lance," I told him.

"Do you throw it like a javelin?" he asked.

"No, ninny," I said, "you strike with it: so." And I thrust my lance into a tree.

He was not impressed. "My javelins are better, then," he said. And quick as thought he reached for one and set it winging into the blue sky, and brought down a bird.

I asked him again where we were, but he just gazed at my shield, and said again, "What's that?"

"A shield," I told him, "to protect me from javelins such as yours."

"Thank goodness the birds don't have those," he said, "or I'd have to give up hunting."

The boy was beside himself with his excitement. He took us to his home - a simple mud hut - to meet his mother.

I have not seen on any human countenance such sadness as I traced in the lines of Perceval's mother's face. She seemed in mourning for the whole of creation. And when she saw her son with five knights, all the colour drained from her. She looked sick and grey.

"Look, mother!" said the lad. "Five knights! I thought they were angels."

His mother said, "Now you have met knights, you will be among angels soon enough."

"I don't know what you're talking about," said Perceval.

"Your father and your two brothers were knights," said Perceval's mother. "Ravens glutted on their bodies, and pecked out the dear bright jewels of their eyes."

"I will slay the ravens with my javelin," said Perceval. "I don't care. I will go and be a knight, and risk what grief may come."

Perceval fetched an old mule from behind the hut, and mounted it, and would not be dissuaded from coming along with us to Camelot. At last his mother told him, "If you must go, you must. But promise me to honour the ladies you meet. You may kiss them if they let you, and accept a ring from their finger, but you should always be guided by worthy men, and go to church."

"What is church?" asked Perceval.

"Where men serve God, who made the world and put men and women on it," his mother answered.

And with that we left, with Perceval tagging along after us. As we rode away, I could hear his mother keening her sorrow.

I'm afraid none of us took Perceval very seriously that day: a poor lad astray in his wits, we thought him. Our horses soon outpaced his mule. We left him far behind, thinking he would soon tire of his game, and go home to his mother.

But Perceval did not turn back. He followed our tracks till he came to a rich pavilion, which he entered. He helped himself to food and drink and, when a woman appeared, he helped himself to a kiss too, and a ring from her finger, because he thought that was what his mother had told him to do. She struggled when he kissed her, but he only held her tighter, telling her that her kiss was sweeter than the sour lips of his mother's maid.

Perceval continued on his way, till at last he came to Camelot. There he found a scene of great commotion: for a knight in red had just entered the court, rudely seized a cup of wine from the king's hand and dashed its contents over the queen, then left as quickly as he had come. The affront was so odd and unexpected that no one had thought to pursue him.

So when Perceval came in, no one paid him much attention. But he found the king, and said to him, "Make me a knight, and give me arms like those others."

The king was deep in thought, and did not reply. But Sir Kay said, "The king will give you the arms of the red knight who has just stolen a cup from him, if you will fetch them."

It was a cruel joke, but Perceval took it seriously. He set off at once after the red knight. As he left the court, a girl who had been there a whole year without speaking said, "Welcome, brave knight." Sir Kay gave the girl a fierce slap on the cheek, saying, "You're a dumb drab speaking to a dumb lout."

Perceval left the court, and I followed him. I was worried for his safety. He caught up with the red knight, and hallooed to him to stop. "What do you want?" asked the knight.

"The cup you stole from King Arthur," said Perceval, "and your arms, for King Arthur has promised them to me."

"Insolent wretch," growled the knight, and caught

58

Perceval a heavy blow with his lance, rocking the lad on his mule.

Before I could interfere, Perceval had let loose his javelin, and pierced the red knight right through the eye, and killed him. Perceval got down and started to try to strip the body of its armour, but he hadn't the first idea how to set about it. "I'll have to cut this knight up to get him out of his clothes," he said.

He was quite capable of it.

I dressed Perceval in the arms and armour of the red knight, mounted him on the red knight's horse and made him a knight. He gave me the cup the red knight had stolen. "Give this to the king," he said. "I'm off to be a knight. Tell the girl who spoke to me, I shall get even with the man who slapped her." With that he rode off, and there was nothing I could do to stop him.

Perceval rode for many miles deep into the forest, till he met an old grey-haired, straight-backed man who called out to him, "Perceval!"

Perceval stopped. "I am your uncle, the Hermit King," the old man said. "Come with me, and I will teach you how to be a knight."

This must be one of the worthy men my mother told me of, thought Perceval, and he followed the Hermit King to his castle. There, Perceval's uncle taught him how to use the weapons he had won, and how to behave like a knight. "Most of all," said the Hermit King, "avoid loose talk. To speak without need is the mark of a fool. For words rightly used are the magic by which man comes to know the truth."

Then Perceval left his uncle the Hermit King and rode across the country seeking adventures. He conquered many knights, and sent them to Arthur's court, and each one brought a message for the girl whom Kay had slapped: "I will avenge your hurt." Sir Kay laughed it

off, but as the stream of defeated knights poured into
Camelot, his laugh took on a hollow, uneasy ring.

One day, Perceval came to a river, flowing fast and cold
and deep. The only way across was a bridge as thin as
a needle and sharp as a sword edge, like the bridge which
the girl made in the old story from a hair of her head.
A man of sense would have turned back: but Perceval
was not a man of sense. He led his horse out and the
instant he stepped on to the bridge, it was wide enough
for a cart to cross.

Then he came to a second river, flowing fast and cold
and deep. The only way across was a bridge of ice. The
sun shone through it and broke in colours on the water;
it seemed a bridge to cross in dreams, not solid enough
to bear the weight of day. But Perceval stepped on to it,
and once again the illusion vanished, and the bridge
became solid and strong.

Then he came to a third rushing river, whose banks
were linked by a stout stone bridge, with marble columns
along its sides each topped with a ball of gold. Perceval
stepped across, and found himself in an orchard of
withered apple trees. In the orchard stood a castle.

Perceval entered the castle. The hall was hung with rich
purple tapestries, and a bed stood there covered with a
gold cloth. On the bed was a man, the very image of
Perceval's uncle the Hermit King. But where the Hermit
King was upright and strong, this man lay back weakly
as if severely wounded; it was as if all the blood had seeped
from his body. This was Perceval's other uncle, the
Maimed King. It was all he could do to motion Perceval
to take a seat.

When Perceval sat down, a maiden walked through the
hall carrying a lance. Though it was wooden, blood
welled from the lance's tip like tears. After this came a
bald maiden, carrying a golden chalice from which a pure

intense light shone. Perceval was very curious about his uncle, and the bleeding lance, and the chalice, but he remembered the Hermit King's advice about not talking too freely, so he did not ask about them.

Then Perceval heard a horn sound, and a voice cry out, "Let the stranger go!" The Maimed King motioned him away, and Perceval left the castle and remounted his horse. Immediately, the horse bolted, carrying him away at a fierce gallop across the first bridge. All around him thunder crashed and lightning whipped across the sky. The rain was so heavy the paths were running with water, and the earth turned to mud and sludge.

Perceval's horse could barely keep upright, and he could not control it. It was in a lather of fear, and would not stop till it had crossed the third bridge. There, Perceval found himself in a pleasant meadow, where the sun shone and the flowers swayed in the lightest of breezes. Across the river, the sky was still dark, and growing darker.

Perceval rode away, none the wiser for what had happened. And as he rode, he met up with a poor woman on a broken-down mangy old nag, that was really only fit for dog's meat. The woman might have been pretty, but you couldn't tell, for she was filthy and scarred. When she saw him, she tried to pull the rags of her clothing across her body to cover her skin, but as soon as she closed one rent, another gaped. Her face and body had been cruelly whipped by the rain and scorched by the sun.

Perceval spoke a blessing to her, and she answered, "Thank you for your greeting. I wish you all your heart desires, although it is you who are responsible for my sorry life."

"But I have never seen you before," said Perceval.

"You have," replied the woman. "You kissed me, and took my ring, and when my husband, the Proud Knight of the Heath, found out what had happened, he beat me, and now forces me to ride ahead of him in misery and torment, in the same clothes I wore that day. I don't know what pleasure it gives him, to see me suffer; I wish he would let me die."

"I will stay and tell him that you did no wrong," said Perceval.

"Do not wait," said the woman, "for my husband will surely kill you. He kills any man who talks to me; one lies gutted only a few miles back. Go on your way."

Just then the Proud Knight arrived, riding across the land like a storm, and bellowing, "How dare you speak to my wife? You shall die for that! I can't trust her with anyone: it's not so long ago that she entertained a coarse Welsh youth in my pavilion, let him eat my pies and drink my wine, and gave him a ring, and a kiss, and who knows what else besides."

"I am that coarse youth," said Perceval, "and you are an idiot. I took the kiss and the ring without your wife's consent, because I knew no better, and I am sorry for it. You are wrong to punish her."

"By God, you've the face to admit it!" spluttered the Proud Knight, and the two went at each other for all they were worth. But the Proud Knight was no match for Perceval, and soon he was begging for mercy. Perceval told him he must take his wife to the nearest castle, and there bathe her and care for her till she was her old self again. Then he must take her to King Arthur and confess how badly he had treated her. He told him, also, to tell the girl whom Kay had slapped that she was not forgotten.

When the Proud Knight came to King Arthur's court, he brought the first news of Perceval for some weeks. King Arthur very much wanted to meet the lad who was doing such great deeds, and he determined to go and seek him out. "I'll not rest another two nights in one bed till I've found him, said the King."

We searched high and low for Perceval, but could not come across him. Then one day, Sir Kay saw a knight standing in a dream by the drifted snow and went to question him. "Hoy, you!" he shouted, and got no further. The strange knight, disturbed from his private thoughts, struck Sir Kay with his lance, and broke his arm in three places. Then he returned to his daydream.

I knew it could only be Perceval. I approached him cautiously, like a hunter stalking a deer, and stood by him quietly till he looked up. "Why, Sir Gawain," he said, "good day. I don't suppose you saw a ruffian who disturbed me just now; I chased him off. I was just looking at these drops of blood in the snow - from some injured bird I suppose - and thinking of the girl who spoke so kindly to me at King Arthur's court, and the blow Sir Kay gave her, bringing red into her white cheek."

"That was Sir Kay just now," I said. "You have broken his arm."

"I am glad of it," said Perceval.

What a feast we made of it that night, boy! But Perceval would not return to Camelot with us: he still wanted to roam the land, looking for adventures. Or perhaps he realised already that the adventure he was in was an adventure without end.

VIII

The Quest for the Holy Grail

I'll leave Perceval for a while, and tell you what happened when we returned to Camelot after finding him. It's all part of his story really, but he wasn't there.

A maiden on a snow-white mule was waiting at the gates of Camelot. The mule's harness glittered with precious stones, and the girl's silken dress shimmered and shone. She wore a head-dress of gold, and around her neck hung a shield bearing a red cross. She had a white dog with her.

She sang:

"Lully, lullay, lully, lullay,
The falcon has borne my mate away.

He bore him up, he bore him down,
He bore him into an orchard brown.

In that orchard there is a hall,
That is hung with purple and pall.

And in that hall there is a bed,
That is hung with gold so red.

And in that bed there lies a knight,
His wounds bleeding day and night.

By that bed's side there kneels a maid,
And she weeps both night and day.

And by that bed's side there stands a stone,
'Corpus Christi' written thereon.

Lully, lullay, lully, lullay,
The falcon has borne my mate away."

She said, "There is a riddle for you to read, King Arthur. Until it is solved, the Maimed King will never recover his health, the trees in his orchard will never blossom or fruit, and I will never recover my golden hair."

As she spoke she flung back her head-dress, and showed that she was entirely bald. Her head was as smooth and bare as polished ivory.

"One of your knights has already failed us," she said. She took the shield from around her neck. "Hang this shield with the red cross on a pillar in this hall. My dog will guard it, and will not bark or move till the knight who is worthy of it comes."

The king took the shield from her, and hung it where she showed him. Then he asked her to speak more clearly about what was to come.

"This is the quest of the Holy Grail," she said. "The Grail is the most precious of all holy relics, and you must seek it out, or all this land will be laid waste. And before you start, from that Grail you shall be fed." Then she departed.

That evening, as we were seated in the hall, there was a great thunderclap, and then all the room was filled with light, and the scent of all the spices of the East. A vessel appeared before us, borne by no visible hand, covered with a white cloth that we might not see it. And from that vessel every knight was fed with what meat he most desired.

When the vision was gone, we all fell on our knees. I spoke for every man, when I told the king, "Lord, this is the greatest mystery we shall ever know. Tonight the holy vessel that fed us was covered from our sight. I shall not rest till I have seen it plain, and the riddle sung to us by the bald maiden has been explained."

All the knights of the Round Table went in search of the Holy Grail, and the court of the Maimed King. But – I see now – we went about it the wrong way. We thought we could fight our way to grace; which is like asking a mapmaker to draw the way to heaven.

In any event, I spent months scouring Britain for the Maimed King, but had no luck. I had more or less given up when I came to the castle of a man called Tybaut. Tybaut gave me shelter on my way, though that day he had suffered severely in a tournament with Meliant de Lis, a young knight whom he had brought up in his own house. Meliant was in love with Tybaut's eldest daughter, a spiteful, malicious girl, who had set her love against her father for the fun of seeing them fight it out. Meliant had youth and the energy of love on his side, and the first day had gone badly for Tybaut.

I had an opportunity to feel the eldest daughter's tongue for myself, for I arrived before the tournament finished, and tethered my horse to an oak tree to watch what was going on. I was sick of travelling and sick of fighting, and beginning, too, to realise that I could not bludgeon my way to the Grail Castle, so I took no part in the fighting. All the time I could hear Tybaut's eldest daughter rattling on about Meliant's wonderful qualities - *such* a neat figure on his horse, *so* valiant, *really* the most perfect knight there had ever been - and I could see her younger sister, who was called the Girl with the Little Sleeves because of the dresses she wore, getting more and more fed up. Finally, the Girl with the Little Sleeves said, "Meliant's not fit to polish the armour of a certain knight *I* could tell you of."

"You're just jealous," said the older sister. "How dare you say that?" And she struck the Girl with the Little Sleeves full in the face, so that the marks of her fingers stood out on the tender flesh. Then, to calm herself, she started to jeer at me, preferring to believe I was some vagabond only pretending to be a knight, because I would not fight.

That evening, the Girl with the Little Sleeves begged me to be her champion against her sister. "What on earth can I do, child?" I said, for she was little more than a child.

"My sister kept on and on about how Meliant was the best knight who ever lived," she said, "and having seen you by the oak tree, I knew it wasn't true. So I told her so, and she hit me, and called me jealous, which wasn't nice, and I think she ought to get what's coming to her. She can boast, but I tell her, bantams will crow."

I couldn't help laughing, and I agreed to be her knight on the next day.

The next day I wore her sleeve on my helmet as a token I was her knight, and took the side of Tybaut against Meliant. When Meliant entered the field, I heard the elder daughter crying, "Ladies, here he comes, Meliant de Lis, the prince of all knights!" So I settled my lance and charged him.

He was a game one, Meliant, I'll grant him. But all the same I gave him a tumble, and I did enjoy delivering his horse to the Girl with the Little Sleeves as her prize. You should have heard those two loving sisters set to: the action on the field was nothing to it. The Girl with the Little Sleeves compared Meliant flat on the ground in his heavy armour to a black beetle struggling with its legs in the air; her sister called her a wily scheming little hussy; and neither of them would have had much hair left if their maids hadn't pulled them apart.

When I left, the Girl with the Little Sleeves held on to my stirrup, and looked up at me so fetchingly you'd never have believed it wàs the same girl who'd been scrapping with her sister not an hour before. She kissed my foot. "What was that for?" I asked.

"So you won't forget me," she said.

"My hair will be grey before I forget you," I told her. It's greying now, but I've still not forgotten. And I've not forgotten, either, what happened next.

I told you I'd really given up the Grail Quest. I was just wandering aimlessly. And just when I'd decided there was no hope, I came to a cold fierce-running river, and the only way across the river was the needle bridge sharp as a sword-edge. I crossed that bridge, and the bridge of ice, and the bridge of stone, and I came to the orchard of withered trees, and the Grail Castle. I knew deep inside me I'd found what I'd given up looking for.

At the Grail Castle, I saw the Maimed King in his gold bed, and weeping at its foot, the bald maiden who had come to Camelot. And I met there twelve knights, each a hundred years old, though they looked only forty, and dined with them. When we sat down, a maiden appeared carrying the lance from which blood was dripping, and the bald maiden carrying the golden Grail. The Grail fed us, each according to our desire, and as I looked at it, sometimes it seemed to be a metal vessel, and sometimes a little child. And in the air behind the maidens I thought

I saw a crowned king nailed to a cross, with a spear thrust in his side. The twelve knights cried out to me to speak, before it was too late, but I had no voice to speak with. I felt the agony of those nails in my own flesh, and I could not say a word.

The next I remember, they were all gone, and I was alone, with a chessboard before me. One set of pieces was ivory, and the other was gold. I moved an ivory piece, idly, and a gold piece moved against me of its own accord. Three times I played; three times I lost. At the third checkmate, I too heard a horn sound, and a voice cry "Let the stranger go!", and had to leave the castle. On me, too, the heavens opened, till I was safe across the needle bridge.

I knew there was nothing more I could do to pursue the Grail Quest: I too, had failed. I took the road for Camelot, to see if anyone had come to claim the shield that the bald maiden had left.

Only one other knight of all those who set out to seek it came to the Grail Castle: Lancelot. But when he came, he was not fed. No Grail appeared. He had mixed and drunk his own cup of pleasure; at the court of the Maimed King he swallowed its bitter dregs.

IX

The Holy Grail

As for Perceval, he had forgotten God.

His mother told him always to go to church; but he did not, and he was more lost than any of us. As yet he knew nothing of the bald maiden, nor her riddle, nor the Holy Grail. He just wandered across the country, till he came to the castle of the Queen of the Circle of Gold.

Along the way to this castle, Perceval passed dead and dying knights whose armour was black with scorch marks; they seemed to have been roasted alive. But it was not his way to question what he saw, and he carried on his way. The castle stood in a meadow, at a place where three rivers meet, and it turned round in the wind faster than the eye could follow. On its battlements were cunning archers made of copper, that fired darts sharp enough to pierce the sharpest armour. Inside the castle, its queen guarded the crown of thorns from Christ's head, set in a circle of gold.

72

Perceval rode unharmed through the hail of darts, and struck the door of the revolving castle three times with his sword. Immediately it stopped turning, and the copper archers dropped their bows. Perceval was a man free from the evil thoughts that eat away a man's soul, and no magic had power against him.

The queen of the castle received Perceval with all honour. She took the Circle of Gold containing the crown of thorns and set it on his head. He remembered God, and crossed himself, and made confession to the Queen of the Circle of Gold. She then told him his task was to cure his uncle the Maimed King, by asking the meaning of the mystery of the Grail and the bleeding lance. "But first," she said, "you must go to the court of King Arthur and collect a shield which awaits you there, with a red cross on it. That will not be easy, for all the land about my castle has been laid waste by the Knight of the Burning Dragon. He is a tall knight with a scarred face. Folk say he got those scars in a tussle with the Devil, from whom he won his magic shield with a dragon's head, and with this he scorches men and women to death. He kills for pleasure."

"The sooner I meet him, the sooner I defeat him," said Perceval, and he departed at once from the castle of the Queen of the Circle of Gold.

It was not long before the Knight of the Burning Dragon saw Perceval riding alone through the blackened landscape. The Knight snorted his contempt for such a puny figure, drew his sword, and charged. Perceval lowered his lance.

A blast of fire from the dragon's head burnt Perceval's lance down to the fist, and then the Knight of the Burning Dragon was on him, striking downwards with his keen-edged sword. Perceval parried the blow, and quickly sliced down with his own sword, splitting the terrible shield right down to the dragon's head. When he withdrew it, flames were flickering up and down the blade, wrapping it in deadly fire. He thrust it into the dragon's mouth.

In its death agonies, the dragon's head twisted and writhed; at the last, it turned upon its master, and with its final breath burnt him to ashes.

Perceval rode on unmolested to Camelot.

I saw him arrive, and take down the shield with the red cross. The dog that the bald maiden had left broke into frantic barking as he lifted it down, as the maiden had foretold, and so we knew the shield was meant for him.

As the next day dawned, a ship came sailing up to the castle in the early morning mist. There was no one aboard save an old white-haired man who sat in silence at the tiller, gazing out to sea. Perceval stepped into the ship and it moved away, though there was not a breath of wind to fill its silken sails.

In that ship Perceval and the ancient steersman sailed in silence for more days and nights than they could count, till they were out of reach of the knowledge of man, on a strange sea under stranger stars. There they came to an island, and on it they heard four horns sounding from a four-cornered castle. They pulled the ship its own length up the smooth white sand. Perceval walked up to the castle, but the steersman stayed with his boat, gazing out to sea.

In the castle courtyard by a crystal fountain was a branching apple tree. On the sand beside the fountain sat two men with long white beards who greeted Perceval by name, and kissed his shield. "This was Joseph of Arimathea's shield," they said. "We knew him, long ago, before the Crucifixion. It was he who brought the Holy Grail to Britain."

Perceval and the two old men went in to eat. Everything was of the finest. In the middle of the meal, a golden crown on a long chain appeared, falling slowly through the air, and the floor of the great hall opened to reveal a dark pit, from which came a great sound of moaning and weeping. The golden crown hovered over the pit until the meal was finished, and then it disappeared.

"Tell me," said Perceval, "what is the meaning of these things?"

"If you had asked that question of your uncle the Maimed King, much sorrow could have been prevented," said the two old men. "We will explain the crown and the pit to you, if you promise to return here when you can."

Perceval promised. They told him that the crown meant he was to be king of that island, the Isle of Plenty, and of the place beneath it, the Isle of Need, whose people he had heard crying. "Here you must bring the Grail, which will feed and comfort those poor souls below."

So Perceval set out once more across the ridges of the sea, with the silent steersman. This time, however, he took no weapons with him. "I have done with fighting," he said.

He landed at the very place where the Maimed King's castle stood, and again crossed the three bridges and entered its hall. The Maimed King still lay suffering on his bed, with the bald maiden kneeling at its foot.

Once again Perceval saw the lance dripping blood, and the glowing Grail. This time he bowed his head and fell to his knees. "Tell me," he said, "whom does the Grail serve? Why does the lance bleed? And what is the cause of your suffering?"

The Maimed King said, "The lance is the lance with which the Roman centurion Longinus pierced Our Lord's side as he hung on the cross, and the Grail is the vessel in which His precious blood was caught. I have been its guardian since my uncle, Joseph of Arimathea, brought it here, and all this time it has fed and sustained me. I have been maimed since a knight called Balin came to this castle and, in a fury, struck me through the thighs with the lance of Longinus. Since that time no crops have grown on the land I rule. Only now that you have asked these questions can I find relief, and the land revive. The Grail is now yours to guard."

Perceval took the lance of Longinus, and held it so that a drop of blood fell from its tip into each of the Maimed King's wounds, and they healed as if they had never been. Then the Maimed King was maimed no more, and he rose in his age with the strength of his youth, and looked Perceval straight in the eyes. "My thanks, nephew, for this mercy," he said.

Perceval then told him all the strange things that had happened to him, as I have told them to you. And the bald maiden gave the Grail into Perceval's keeping, and her hair grew long and full and golden.

Perceval stepped through the orchard of trees bursting into blossom, and took ship again, and sailed away with the ancient steersman: some say, to the Isle of Plenty. No one has ever seen him or heard from him again; and with him, the Grail too passed from the world of mortal men.

X

Lancelot and Guinevere

Well, boy, that was the quest of the Holy Grail. I never understood half of it. I don't believe Perceval did, either. It was because he didn't try to understand that he succeeded. He just accepted what came. He was a very simple man.

What I did understand was that that quest meant the end of our old way of living. All the fighting, and the jousting, and the feasting. It had lost its tang. Those of us who came back from the Grail quest were like a lot of lost sheep. We knew we ought to live differently, but we didn't know how to. We kept on with our Round Table and our tournaments simply because we couldn't think of any other way to behave.

I think it was worst of all for Lancelot. Everyone had thought he would find the Grail. He'd been the best knight in the world since he was just a boy; and he was a merciful, a kindly man. Yet it was Perceval who was chosen; Lancelot was judged unworthy.

It was then the trouble between him and the queen began. They always loved each other, I think. Did you ever hear, boy, how on the day the king knighted Lancelot, Lancelot was so shy he lost his sword, and Guinevere found it for him, and brought it to him wrapped in her mantle? He dedicated it to her at that moment, and - give him his due - he has never failed her, in right or in wrong.

Lancelot was never like the other young knights. There was always something ... *unworldly* about him. Most of us, you know, live from day to day; we make our bargains with life as we go along. Lancelot was never like that. He lived for an ideal of knighthood, of friendship, of loyalty. He could be so fierce, and so still, all at the same time. Once you've seen Lancelot explode onto the battlefield you know that most fighting is just a children's game of touch-as-touch-can. Yet I never knew him lose his temper, nor raise his voice or his fist to one who could not defend himself. Not till this trouble of ours came upon us, and unhinged him, and made him turn on my family.

Anyway, Lancelot lived for his idea of honour. It was a sore test for him that even as he offered his allegiance to the king, his mind was on the fresh young queen who'd found his sword for him. He knew she was the one woman for him, and the one woman he was forbidden even to think of. So he took off on that series of adventures that minstrels thrill the world's courts with night after night; you know the stories as well as I, I'm sure, and I'll not bore you with them now. There was no danger too great, no life harsh enough for him. He thought, you see, to ride out his love, as a man will fight and defeat a fever. But every time he returned to Camelot, Guinevere was there. He would stop a few days, ill at ease, and then set off again. I rode with him sometimes, and I can tell you he did not spare himself. I never saw anyone withstand him; and I never saw anything calm the hungry look he carried in his eyes.

Who knows what passed between the queen and him in those days? All I know is that he blamed his guilty passion for his failure in the great quest of our day, and when he returned, with the stain of travel outside and the stain of defeat inside, he kept away from the queen. He wanted to be free of sin; to be the best knight in the world still. And it worked.

You've seen a burly, fit-looking man with a black beard riding with Lancelot, Sir Urré? Well, when Sir Urré arrived at Camelot he was little more than a skeleton covered in foul, weeping wounds. He had killed a knight called Sir Alpheas at a tournament in Spain, and Sir Alpheas' mother, who was a witch, cast a spell on Urré that his wounds would never heal till they were touched by the best knight in all the world.

We were his last hope, and every knight in Arthur's court touched Sir Urré's wounds trying to cure him. I touched him, and the king did too. Only Lancelot hung back. The king told him he must try, and Lancelot said, "When so many good knights have tried and failed, it would be a sin of pride in me to follow them. I would be ashamed to touch that knight, hoping to prove myself better than my fellows."

"Nevertheless," said the king, "touch him you must, for I have promised that we shall all try."

So Sir Lancelot touched Sir Urré's wounds, and as his fingers passed over the flesh it became whole and healthy.

Then King Arthur and Sir Urré and all the court knelt down and gave thanks to God, but Sir Lancelot made no move. I saw his face, and he was crying: crying like a whipped child.

It was after that that Guinevere sent him away. They

were destroying each other. It was all she could do. But it meant he was far from her when her trouble came.

The trouble was all to do with me, as it turned out. There was a knight called Avarlan who had a grudge against me, and one night he poisoned an apple and set it at the dinner table, knowing my fondness for fruit. But as ill-luck would have it, Guinevere took the apple, and gave it to another knight, Patrise. When Patrise bit into it, his lips turned black. The sound that came from his throat I hope never to hear again: a grating, rasping choke as if he were breathing flame. He died on the spot. There was nothing we could do to save him.

No one said anything, but next day Patrise was in his tomb, and on the tomb were words reading, "Here lies Patrise, the brother of Mador de la Porte, whom the queen killed with poison."

Now the day after that a great tournament was held at Camelot, and the queen waited, no doubt, for Lancelot to arrive, and defend her against the enemies who accused her of Patrise's murder. But Lancelot never came. Instead, Mador de la Porte arrived, and saw his brother's tomb. Mador went straight to the king and demanded justice. He renounced his titles and his lands, and his loyalty to the king. He asked only for Guinevere's death. If she denied the charge, he would prove her guilt in combat with any knight who would champion her. Now this Mador was a good knight, the sort of man Arthur needed as a friend. So the king had no choice but to let Mador's accusation stand, and require the queen to answer it. She denied it, of course. And much later, when Avarlan admitted that it was he who had poisoned the apple, intending it for me, her innocence was made clear to all. But at the time, many thought she had treacherously slain Sir Patrise. Guinevere was not well liked at that time. She was miserable, poor woman, and many of us felt the lash of her tongue. She missed Lancelot: but she had sent him away. And because of that, Lancelot's kindred were cold and resentful to her, just when she needed friends most.

But it was to them she turned – to Lancelot's cousins Bors and Lionel, and his young brother Ector – when the king in his justice gave her forty days to prepare her defence, and find a champion, and Lancelot did not appear to help her. She got cold comfort from them. Bors is a man of strict mind: he told her she was getting what she deserved. She went down on her knees to him to beg his help, and the king found her like that. And then he said the worst thing he could: "What is wrong with you," he asked, "that you cannot keep Sir Lancelot on your side?" Then the king too begged Bors to take Guinevere's part, "for I am certain she is untruly defamed". And Bors agreed to fight on her behalf, if no better knight could be found.

When the day of judgement came, Sir Bors was as good as his word, and readied himself to fight with Mador; but few doubted what the outcome would be. Sir Mador was a strong man, filled with the fury of grief and loss, and Sir Bors an over-dainty fighter, in a cause he doubted.

Bors delayed as long as he could, but when Sir Mador came into the field with his shield on his shoulder and his spear in his hand, and rode about the place crying to King Arthur, "Bid your champion come forth if he dares!" Bors armed himself to fight.

Bors was in the saddle when there came from a wood behind the field a knight on a white horse, carrying arms and bearing a strange shield, riding hard and fast. The horse's coat was flecked with sweat. The knight came to Sir Bors, and said, "Fair knight, withdraw. This battle should be mine."

Then Sir Bors rode to the king and told him a strange knight had come to fight for the queen.

Sir Mador and the strange knight couched their spears and rode together with all their might. Sir Mador's spear splintered to pieces, but the stranger's spear held, and brought Sir Mador, horse and all, tumbling to the dust. Then Sir Mador drew his sword, and the strange knight dismounted and did likewise, and they moved eagerly to battle. This way, that way they moved, each seeking to break through the other's guard. The air rang with the clash of sword on sword. But Sir Mador was a heavy man, who relied on quick victory over his opponents. The strange knight was nimble on his feet, and soon Sir Mador grew weary. And then the stranger delivered such savage blows to Sir Mador's head that Sir Mador was thrown flat and grovelling on the ground, and the stranger unlaced Mador's helm to cut his throat if he did not yield.

And then the stranger spoke, and it was Lancelot's voice. "Mador, you are a dead man, if I will it. Do you retract your wild and malicious claim against the queen, and agree that no mention of it shall remain on Sir Patrise's tomb?"

Mador said, "I do," and the whole court cheered, because Lancelot was back and the queen was reprieved, and the sun had come from behind the clouds and shone on Lancelot's helm till he dazzled all eyes with the majesty of his strength and mercy.

I confess there were tears in my own eyes that day. But through them I could see, apart from the cheering crowd, two dark figures in the shadow, and my heart misgave me. It was my brother Agravaine, and my half-brother Mordred, and they were not smiling.

Mordred: I tell you, that name is like a bad taste in my mouth. I dare say it's not his fault, for his conception was vicious and his upbringing was worse, but there is something maimed and dangerous about Mordred that fills me with fear; and you know, boy, no one has ever called me coward. His eyes creep sideways as he talks, and you can read nothing in them. He is forever asking questions, but I never knew him listen to an answer. He hears and sees only what he wants to. I have seen Mordred when he thinks himself unobserved: it is as if he does not exist. He feeds off the energy of others; he has none of his own. All he has, working in the depth of his bones, is our mother's ill-wishing to King Arthur and all he cherishes. When I saw Mordred draw Agravaine apart that day, and whisper some poison in his ear, and Agravaine's brow furrow and grow dark, I trembled inside. For Agravaine was not a thinker. He was a follower. And though he was a worthy man, he too was nurtured on my mother's magic, and there was that in him that Mordred's subtlety could bind to any evil purpose.

But Mordred was new to court then, and made no open move against Lancelot or the queen. He just bided his time, waiting for the moment to strike.

Lancelot no longer sought to escape from Arthur's court: there were no more wanderings, no more adventures. He remained at Camelot, and soon all the gossips knew that he and the queen were lovers. They scarcely bothered to be discreet: they were too old and too tired for that. The king too must have known what was going on; but to know and to confront knowledge is not the same thing.

Then one day I was with my brothers in the king's chamber, waiting for the king. I could feel in Mordred a tension, a gloating suppressed excitement I had not come across before. Agravaine had a dull face, heavy with decision. I asked him, "Why so gloomy, Agravaine?" and he said, "How can I hold up my head? How can any of us, when we stand by and see our noble king put to shame by Sir Lancelot and the queen?"

That was the line Mordred had fed him. I told him to
hold his tongue; and Gareth and Gaheris, God rest them,
told him even if he spoke they would not hear him. But
he would not keep silence. I begged him to think what
he was doing, but he was ever a stubborn man when he
was set on course; he had not the strength to change his
own mind. "Come what may," he said, "I will disclose
it to the king." Yet he knew as well as I, he owed his
own life to Sir Lancelot. The best of us would have been
full cold at the heart root were it not for Lancelot.

And when the king came in, Agravaine burst out with
his news that was no news, mouthing the words Mordred
had chosen for him, though he thought he had picked
them himself. "My lord," he said, "as your nephew, I
cannot remain silent. I must tell you what all the court
knows, and all the world whispers, to your shame and
our dishonour: Sir Lancelot and Queen Guinevere are
lovers. We can prove them untrue, and traitors to your
person."

The king was so still. I have never seen him so still.

Mordred said, "When you go hunting tomorrow, send
news that you will not return the same night. We shall
surprise them together. Will you take that as proof?"

The king's voice was low, and as steady as if what was
happening did not concern him at all. "I would take that
as proof," he said, "if any of you lived to tell the tale."

On the next day, the king went hunting as planned,
and sent the message. That night Mordred and Agravaine
took twelve other knights and rapped with a spear at the
door of the queen's chamber. "Come out, traitor knight,"
they shouted.

Lancelot was naked. No armour, shield, sword or spear
did he have. He took the queen in his arms, and kissed
her, and called her his special good lady, and he moved
to the door. Mordred and his knights were battering at

it with a wooden bench. "Leave off your noise," shouted Sir Lancelot, "and I will let you in."

"Open the door, then," they replied.

Lancelot unbarred the door, and opened it just wide enough to admit one man, Sir Colgrevance of Gore. Colgrevance blundered in, swinging at Lancelot with his sword. Lancelot slammed the door shut, dodged the blow, tripped Colgrevance and slit his throat with his own knife. He re-barred the door, and then he stripped the body and put on Colgrevance's armour.

Mordred and Agravaine called again for him to come out, but he answered, "You will not take me this night. Take my advice, and leave while you still can."

Sir Lancelot opened the door again. His first stroke took my brother's life. It was a mean end, boy, and Agravaine was not a bad man. But I had warned him not to pick an argument he could not win. The knights fell to Lancelot's sword like corn to the reaper. He killed them all, except the weasel, Mordred, who ran away.

Lancelot wanted to take the queen away with him then, and if he had done so perhaps all this mess could have been sorted out. But she would not go. She could not believe that the king would take heed of Mordred. She did not know, you see, that Mordred was the king's son. So Lancelot took all his kin and the knights who owed him allegiance - a hundred and forty of the strongest knights of King Arthur's court - and rode away to his castle of Joyous Gard, which he renamed Dolorous Gard. My brother Gareth wanted to go with him, he loved Lancelot so. But Lancelot would not allow it, and now I see he must already have been plotting his revenge on my family.

I was with the king when Mordred brought the news of what had happened. Mordred had plenty of blood on him, but not a wound that I could see; but he had the body of my brother Agravaine, and the bodies of the twelve knights who followed him, as proof of what he said.

The king said, "The noble fellowship of the Round Table is broken forever. Lancelot and I must fight, and neither of us can win. And now I must put my fair queen to death, for that is the law, and even I am not above it. May Jesus have mercy on us all."

I told him, "Lord, these proofs are not final. Do not be over-hasty; there may be many reasons why Sir Lancelot was with the queen. Perhaps she sent for him to thank him privately for being her champion against Sir Mador de la Porte. Do not believe any evil of these two you love."

"The proofs are final," said the king. "My Guinevere must die."

XI

The Banishment of Lancelot

Put a log on the fire, boy. The smoke makes me cough, but this is a killing cold. Lancelot plays a waiting game. He must laugh as he looks down from his battlements to watch us blow at our hands. But the world has never felt the wind that could freeze my blood now.

I'm coming to the worst part of my tale: the part we're living now. You know, boy, what has happened, but I shall tell you anyway. For I do not understand it. My thoughts give me no rest, and my dreams no peace.

The king moved like a shadow as Guinevere waited for death. I was with him day and night, and I do not believe he spoke a single word after he sealed her fate. He just watched, watched from his window as his men built a fire in the castle yard, and raised an iron stake in the middle of it. He just watched, and I watched with him, as the queen was brought out in her shift and tied to that stake, and fire was kindled to burn her alive for the wrong she had done. And he just watched, and I

89

watched with him, as Lancelot and all his knights fell on Camelot like an owl on its prey, and freed Guinevere, and carried her away.

I had stayed by my uncle's side. Mordred, I've no doubt, had found some safe dark hole from which to watch the fun. But my brothers Gareth and Gaheris were in the yard. They went unarmed, that the queen should know they had no part in Agravaine and Mordred's plots. Gareth worshipped Lancelot; he would not have had him hurt for all the world.

So when Lancelot was gone, and the queen with him, I went down to find my brothers, and share a cup of wine with them. But they had drunk the dark wine of death, and did not know me. Lancelot had killed them. Lancelot killed my brother Agravaine; I did not blame him. He might have killed my brother Mordred; I would have thanked him. But to kill my brothers Gareth and Gaheris: I cannot forgive him. While I am Gawain, I will hate him. When I can stand again, I will fight him.

I no longer care, boy, what is right and what is wrong. I know I must revenge my brothers; their blood calls out for it.

When I knew they were dead, I helped the king gather his troops, and we pursued Sir Lancelot to the Dolorous Gard. For fifteen weeks we camped outside that fortress. No one came out and no one went in. Lancelot spoke to us from the battlements, pleading for peace, and friendship. I told him I would give him the same peace he gave Gareth; the same friendship he showed Gaheris. He swore he never saw them; he would have given his right arm not to have killed them. But I knew he lied: for when did the great Sir Lancelot kill a man in error? "Leave off your babbling," I told him, "and let us ease our hearts in fighting."

But the king, like Lancelot, wanted peace, and when

the Pope told Arthur to take back his queen, he thought he had a chance to bury the quarrel. I have no grudge against Guinevere, and I held my tongue when the king took his army back to Camelot, and Lancelot rode out unmolested from his castle, with a hundred knights dressed in green velvet, carrying an olive branch for peace, with the queen at his side. I held my tongue when Lancelot and Guinevere knelt before the king, and Lancelot said, "Here we are, Lord, by the Pope's command. Here is your lady the queen; she has never shamed you. If any knight, of any degree, save only King Arthur and Sir Gawain, dare say any dishonour of her, I will prove the lie upon his body. My Lord, you have listened to liars, and that is the cause of the war between us." I mind when Lancelot said "liars" he looked at Mordred; but he never caught my eye: he had not the insolence.

The king, as you know, took Guinevere back, with fine words and fine promises. That was his business, and I held my tongue. But when he held out a hand to Lancelot also, then I spoke. "Lancelot," I said. "The king may do as he wishes, but you and I will never agree. You killed three of my brothers and two of them you slew like a traitor and a coward, when they would not bear arms against you."

Lancelot repeated the same old weary lie: "I never saw them, I did not mean to kill them." He reminded me that he himself had made Gareth a knight, when Gareth was little more than a boy, and Sir Kay had laughed at him and called him "Pretty Hands". He said that Gareth was a true knight, courteous, gentle and good – that at least was no lie – and that he had loved Gareth better than any knight of his own blood. Sir Gaheris he called a fine man, whom he had never wished to harm. But I remembered their ravaged bodies in the courtyard: Gareth's hands were not pretty in death, I told him.

The Banishment of Lancelot

Then Lancelot made his offer. He would walk barefoot, he said, the length of Arthur's lands, and every ten miles he would found a monastery in my brothers' memory. Would that bring them back to life? I asked. No, no. I listened to his rambling, his apologies, his subtle phrases, his show of penitence, and it made no difference to me. I told him, "If King Arthur wishes to make peace with you then he will lose my service, for I never shall."

So Lancelot was banished. He took all his men to France, to this castle and estate of Benwick, where he grew up. We followed him, and laid waste all his lands. So here we are, and here we stay. Lancelot can sue for peace – "peace on any terms" he offered – but he will not get it. The king can urge conciliation; I will not allow it.

The king has little taste for this war, I know. When I fought Lancelot, the king looked so grey, and so old, I nearly called it off. He looked as if he could see everyone in the whole world lying dead before him. But I have sworn to my brothers' shades to make their murderer pay for their deaths, if I can.

Lancelot did not want to fight me. I do not think he can have been afraid. Who knows how that man's mind works? But he could not hold out forever. I made him fight me, outside his castle walls, and that should have finished it. I don't pretend to have had the best of it. Thirteen wounds he gave me, and this one in my head the worst of all. He could have killed me. He should have done so. God knows, I could wish he had, and that was an end. He should know I will always pursue him, while I have a spark of life in my body.

XII

Return to England

The king has brought me terrible news, boy. Be quick, pack up my arms. We leave for England on the next tide.

Lancelot? Lancelot can wait.

It is my brother, Mordred. There is nothing he could not soil. He seeks – I can barely say it – he seeks to marry the queen. It is some twisted notion of justice for his mother: Arthur slept with his sister, and begat Mordred; so Mordred will take Arthur's wife, and beget a new king to inherit Arthur's kingdom.

Hurry, boy, hurry. The queen is besieged. Mordred has told the people that their king is dead. God help us, some of them are even glad. He has used his time well. He has given away his father's possessions with a free hand, and asked nothing in return. The fools he has bought think that under Mordred everyone will be rich and no one will have to work. They say that Arthur is forever fighting, that Mordred will give them peace. They think they will live in the land of ease, where the pigs run around with knives and forks in their backs crying "Eat me".

Curse this wound! It makes my head spin when I try to rise. No! Don't help me. I must stand on my own feet. Give me my sword. I must feel its weight in my hand.

XIII

The Death of Gawain

I can hear a stream running, boy, somewhere to the left. My hearing has grown keen. I have never noticed before how many different notes blend into a stream's song. Go to it, and dip a rag into it. You can moisten my lips, to help me finish my story.

Thank you. Thank you, boy. The water is pure. It brings me to my wits, as the forest well did to the enchanter Merlin.

Well, we bloodied Mordred's nose, didn't we? He has cause to fear his father's army now. He thought he could prevent us landing; he thought we had grown old and weak. Now he knows better. Yet his troops are young and disciplined; the king will be hard-pushed when next they meet. And I will not be there to help him. I know my death day has come. I have been hurt again in the same place where Sir Lancelot wounded me.

The water has cleared away the ash taste from my throat. I want you, boy, when I'm dead, to write to Sir

Lancelot. Tell him that King Arthur needs him. Tell him that the queen is in danger. Tell him I forgive him; beg him to pray for my soul. For I see now it is my wilful temper has destroyed this realm. Anger and ill-luck, anger and ill-luck have riven us apart.

Lancelot should be here. Mordred could never stand against him. For Lancelot is the flower of all the noble knights that ever I heard of or saw in all my days; I do believe he killed my brothers by mischance, and spared me in the pity and mercy of his nature so that I could raise my sword once more in the just cause of my king. I am proud that it is his blow that will send me over to that other land. Have them write on my tomb, boy, "Here lies Gawain, whom Lancelot killed through Gawain's foolishness." Then the world will have my name, and my story. When you're alive, boy, never give your name unless it's asked. When you're dead, it doesn't matter.

Tell Lancelot to make all haste.

I was always a hothead. Some found me rough, I know; I once made a man eat with my dogs for a month with his hands tied behind his back for mistreating a girl. But I meant well. Perhaps that's the best any of us can say in the end. What a mess we've made of our lives.

I've unravelled it all for you, boy. I feel better for that. Everything seemed so *right* as it happened, yet all I trace as I look back is the same mistakes being made again and again. It was Merlin who started it all, by giving Uther the shape and face of my grandfather, to seduce Igraine. Then Morgause and Arthur. Guinevere and Lancelot. Mordred and Guinevere. And me.

So many mistakes.

The fog is closing in, boy. I can hear the waves cracking against the rocks. The fog is closing in.

Christ deliver us! Boy, I see strange sights through this mist. I see a battlefield, inland, covered with corpses. Dead

knights litter the bed of the river that flows by, like a shoal of silver fish. I see the king, and I see Mordred.

The king has lifted his spear. Ah! Mordred has taken the spear in his chest. He is pulling the spear through his own body to get at his father. There is a dribble of blood from Mordred's mouth. He is lifting his sword. He strikes!

I do not wish to see any more. Come close, boy. Wet my lips.

I can hear singing. Listen! Do you hear them? Over there, through the mist: such a sad song. A song to rend the fibres of the brain. And yet: my blood sings with it. *This ae night, this ae night, every night and all, fire and fleet and candlelight, and Christ receive thy soul.*

O, the light, the light.

Postscript:

These words did I take down from my lord Gawain in his time of trial. My lord was in a fever and in great pain. Much that he said was confused, and there is some that I do not understand. There is much that does not agree with the other chronicles I have seen. Yet I did not feel it right to alter my lord's words, and I leave them here as he spoke them, to be believed or not.

A bad time is coming. King Arthur is dead, by Mordred's hand, as Sir Gawain foresaw. Some say he will come again to save us from ourselves, but how or when that is to be I do not know. His realm is in ruins. England is made over to the raven and the wolf.

And so for the love I bore Sir Gawain, I leave this record of his life so that all may not be lost in the wreck. May you who read it pray for his soul.

May the Lord have mercy on us all.

Signed under my hand
Niall son of Eian, late squire to Sir Gawain of Orkney

AUTHOR'S NOTE ON SOURCES

The best book on King Arthur was written in the fifteenth century by Sir Thomas Malory. He was translating and adapting from many existing stories - mostly written in French - and he did it so well that his book, usually called *Le Morte D'Arthur*, "The Death of Arthur", has become a classic. Most re-tellings since his day have relied heavily on Malory, and mine is no exception. But I have also tried to draw on some of the rest of the mass of medieval Arthurian literature, from the dimly-seen figure of early Welsh legend to the king of the French courtly romances. The account of Merlin's madness is taken mainly from an Irish story, *The Madness of Sweeney*; the story of Sir Owain is taken from the Welsh *Mabinogion* and a similar story by the French poet Chretien de Troyes. The story of Gawain's marriage is from an English poem, *The Wedding of Sir Gawain* and also from Chaucer's *Wife of Bath's Tale*. The stories of *Sir Gawain and the Green Knight* and *The Fair Unknown* are both from English poems. My account of the Grail Quest is based mainly on the French *High Book of the Grail.* In addition I have taken brief touches, phrases and incidents from many other sources. The best guide to all this medieval material is R.S. Loomis, *Arthurian Literature in the Middle Ages: A Collaborative History;* it should be in all good libraries, as should translations of many of the Arthurian stories and poems it describes. There have, of course, been numerous accounts of King Arthur since Malory, and I have read and benefited from many of them. Two which have been of particular importance to me are John Heath-Stubbs' magnificent long poem, *Artorius,* and T.H. White's brilliant four-volume re-imagining, *The Once and Future King.*

$11.95

DATE			